T0148180

Danger
in Paris

Danger in Paris

A Mystery

Erwin Hargrove

ARCHWAY
PUBLISHING

Copyright © 2015 Erwin C. Hargrove.

All rights reserved. No part of this book may be used or reproduced by any means, graphic, electronic, or mechanical, including photocopying, recording, taping or by any information storage retrieval system without the written permission of the publisher except in the case of brief quotations embodied in critical articles and reviews.

Archway Publishing books may be ordered through booksellers or by contacting:

Archway Publishing
1663 Liberty Drive
Bloomington, IN 47403
www.archwaypublishing.com
1-(888)-242-5904

Because of the dynamic nature of the Internet, any web addresses or links contained in this book may have changed since publication and may no longer be valid. The views expressed in this work are solely those of the author and do not necessarily reflect the views of the publisher, and the publisher hereby disclaims any responsibility for them.

Any people depicted in stock imagery provided by Thinkstock are models, and such images are being used for illustrative purposes only.
Certain stock imagery © Thinkstock.

ISBN: 978-1-4808-1392-2 (sc)
ISBN: 978-1-4808-1393-9 (e)

Library of Congress Control Number: 2014921920

Printed in the United States of America.

Archway Publishing rev. date: 1/27/2015

I dedicate this book to my granddaughters, Blythe Cate and Catherine Hargrove.

Three friends made good suggestions for improving the book: Alex Mcleod, Frank Somerville, and David Bell. I thank Maneli Reihani for guiding me through the editing process.

Chapter 1

This story of unfolding events amazed the participants when it was concluded. What seemed plausible in retrospect was not so at the time, and even after the fact, there were mysteries. People and events in Paris in the 1920s and in Hungary during the Second World War, later in Portugal, and then in the 1980s in Spain, Morocco, and Algeria, all jangled together in matters of theft, treachery, dishonesty, politics, and murder. It was one surprise after another.

In August 1988 John Page and his wife Julie, arrived in Paris for a sabbatical year. John was a professor of history at Vanderbilt University, and Julie, also a professor, was an anthropologist. He worked in the field of modern North African history and she was an anthropologist who did research on women in Islam. They were on research fellowships and were both to be at the Sorbonne.

They knew Paris well, having lived there before, and settled easily into an apartment in the Marais district. It was comfortable with studies for each of them and was near cafes that they had often enjoyed. As they were unpacking books, Julie casually remarked,

"I would be happy just to read for a year, go out to cafes and the theater and see friends and do no work at all."

"You would be restless in a week," he replied, "and besides you want to finish your book."

Julie was writing a book about the theories of the French anthropolgist Claude Levy-Strauss.

And John was finishing a book on Islamist movements in modern North Africa.

They went out dinner that night to an Alsatian restaurant at the opening to the Isle St. Louis. As they were crossing the bridge a juggler dressed as a clown was tossing his balls into the air and performing magical tricks as an appreciative crowd was laughing and applauding. This was Paris. Once in the restaurant, and seated on benches along long tables shared by customers, they recognized many of the waiters wearing their long aprons, who also seemed to remember their faces. This was a rough and ready place to eat ham, cabbage and large hunks f bread, with mugs of cold beer.

Once they had settled in, they called in at their offices at the Sorbonne and called old friends,

John had a mission to perform. He was in search of friends of his mother and her brother, who had lived in

Paris in the 1920s. His moher had died when he was a boy and he was in search of her as well as her life in France. Her friends were named Dubois and their family had a house near Grambois in Provence that he hoped to find. His grandmother had placed his mother's and uncle's letters in a closet on a hall landing of her Louisville house and never disturbed them. John did not find them until his maiden aunt, Sarah Catherine, had recently died. She had never said a word to him about the materials. It took him quite a while but he read all the letters.

His uncle Charles had died in Paris in 1928. John's mother had talked to him about living in France but she had died of pneumonia in 1939, so he new virtually nothing of her life there. He only knew the family name, the general location of the house, and the name of the house itself, Provencal, from the letters. He was anxious to explore his mother's past. He had known many of her friends when he was growing up n Louisville but for reasons that he did not understand he did not ask them about her. His father got sad when John asked him to describe her. His grandmother and aunt were some help but he wanted to know more. So he and Julie went in search of the past.

John's mother, Sally, had lived in Paris in 1926–27. She was a twenty-five-year-old Junior Leaguer from Louisville with time on her hands. Her diary was pretty clear that she was bored with boyfriends, bridge parties, and dances. She was just waiting to get married but could not find the right man. John was glad that she waited, or he would have been someone different. When he came along in 1930, he seemed to fit his mother and father just fine. Sally's older brother, Charles, lived in France from 1921 until 1928. He was something of an architect who had finished his education at the Grand Ecole des Beaux Artes, and devoted his energies to enjoying life. A snide person would have called him a playboy. His aunt Gladys, an affluent widow, took him to France in 1921. She had been to school in Paris as a young girl and had kept her friendships alive. Charles had dallied with college to no purpose for a year or two, but Gladys and her brother, Albert, who was an artist with temperament but little talent, thought that Charles had the makings of an artist. Albert lived with his German wife, Sissa, in various parts of Europe that suited his fancy. There was plenty of money in the family, all of it inherited from their father, a rich banker. John's grandfather, Robert, who ran the family bank, played golf and enjoyed whiskey and cigars, had his feet on the ground but had spoiled his children, especially Sally. He did not understand his son and was happy to see him quietly kidnapped by his sister. Robert's wife, Sarah, was a society lady with lots of respectable, unexciting causes, but she was a warm mother and a sympathetic person. Charles wrote home to her rather than to his father. Aunt Gladys and Uncle Albert did not regard the children's parents as sufficiently cultured to bring them up right. For example, Albert wrote young Charles letters with drawing lessons in them, and both aunt and uncle wrote Sally and Charles about their European travels. They were only high-class tourists, but that fact escaped their pretensions.

Charles' diaries and letters reveal the search for and discovery of a French persona; he had never been happy with his American identity, even as a Southerner, a refuge for some. He worked very hard on his French, writing and speaking, and cultivated only French friends. Charles gradually gravitated to interior architecture or design. His letters suggest that he was not impressed with the quality of instruction, and he seems to have attended classes on and off as it suited him. His letters describe an active social life of dances, luncheons, and parties. Aunt Gladys returned home in 1923 and died soon after, but Charles was no longer reliant on her. John Page presumed that she left him some money because she was childless. His father was not likely to finance him indefinitely, yet he lived comfortably.

Charles had made many friends in Paris by the time that Sally arrived. His diaries and letters describe them as people with titles, perhaps from long ago dynasties or more recent purchases. Viscount Bernard D'Arzy was a particular friend, and his wife, Benoît, was very kind to Sally. Charles's letters also spoke of the Count de Segenzac and Viscount de Pomerau. He eventually became a friend of a Captain Molyneux, a well-known Irish dress designer, who asked Charles to design a house for him. Molyneux enjoyed the good life. For example, Charles and Sally drove with him to Cannes from Paris at Christmas in an open roadster packed with fur robes and picnic baskets.

Sally met an Englishman on the boat who followed her to Paris in her first weeks there, but unfortunately he had no money and the romance faded away. She wrote in her diary that "I might have been Mrs. Ben Adams but it could not be." John would have been a young Ben Adams. It could have been worse. An Italian from Trieste, whom she met on a trip with Charles, declared his love and followed her to Paris. No telling who John would have been from that union. She had not been long in Paris when she wrote her mother about how Charles was out every night with his smart friends and slept late in the mornings. At first they lived in the same small hotel in Montparnasse, but eventually she found other American girls with whom to live and to enjoy Paris on her own. She did find French friends, especially Katie Dubois, whom she had met through Charles. Sally wrote her mother that Katie was teaching her French, and she was teaching Katie the Charleston. Katie's mother was a concert pianist, and her father was in investments of some kind.

Sally wrote her mother about Katie and a family country house in Provence that they called the Provencale. Both Charles and Sally had visited the house and the family there, and John found photographs of them with members of the family: Katie, her parents, and her sister. Katie's mother was very well known and highly regarded in France. But John had only a general idea where the house might be.

He and Julie flew to Aix en Provence, checked into a hotel and the next day set out driving in search of Provencal. They drove to Grambois, and asked a lady in a food market about the Provencal. She gave general and vague directions, so they went farther along until they saw a tiny village on a high hill and drove up there. A few old men were sitting under some shade trees in the center of town. John parked the car and walked over to them. John asked, "Connaissez vous le château Provencal?" The French say "chateau" for a country house. One old fellow in his undershirt and a beret on his head walked him over to one edge of a hill and pointed, "Las bas."

At the bottom of the hill John turned right because he had come from the left, and there upon them was a dirt road and a sign that read Provencale. A short drive led to a clearing where a stone house, surrounded by trees, sat grandly. A dog was chained to a pillar in front of the house, and a sign warned about the dangerous "chien". Directly ahead of them was a short stone wall that bordered on a field behind. John walked toward the wall, went over it, and walked in back of the house in hopes of finding someone. Julie was not keen on this idea but followed as they walked through the meadow.

Three people were sitting in a side yard. John and Julie climbed the wall and John walked toward them, holding a letter in his hand that had the embossed word

"Provencal" on the top of the page. A young man got up and walked to them. John explained in his best French that his mother and uncle had visited the house long ago as friends of the family. The letter was from Katie to his mother. The young man spoke good English, having lived in the United States. John asked him about Katie, and he replied that she was his grandmother, who lived in Paris. "Why don't you call her?" He lived in Lyon and was at Provencal only because it was the May Day holiday and he was meeting with the caretaker and his wife.

John explained that his uncle had designed the theater in the house, and the young man replied that it was not in good condition but was being renovated. That stopped any invitation to see the theater or the house for that matter. His uncle had described the painting of murals on the front of the house, but caution about the dog held him back from asking to see them. He and Julie left through a yard on the other side of the house.

Such was their visit to Provencal. They went back to Paris, and he called Katie. After some confusion about who he was, she remembered his uncle but not his mother. She did remember Sally when they saw her two days later. They had arranged to see her the next day, but when he called then, she asked to meet the following day because she was watching a commemoration of the end of World War Two at St. Paul's Cathedral in London. They later learned that her husband had fought in the Resistance. She was a friend of England and America.

Her grandfather had been an American businessman who had settled in Marseille before World War One and married her grandmother. Provencal was owned by her mother's family. In the morning John bought a bouquet in a flower shop in the Place Vendôme, and they set out for the Bois de Boulogne on the Metro.

They had the address and found a small cluster of elegant two-story apartments but could not find her number. A polite man saw their puzzled wanderings, took John by the arm, and led them to her place just as an older woman walked out with a cocker spaniel on a leash. John decided that she had tired of waiting for them and decided to take the dog out, so he rushed up to her and thrust the bouquet of flowers into her hand. Julie later asked, "How did you know it was Katie?" He didn't know, and yet he did and it was Katie.

Her apartment was rich in furnishings, paintings, and antiques, and they walked through to a sunny garden in the back. She had set a table with bottles of whiskey for the "Anglo-Saxons," but they drank only water. Her English was good, although she said that it was not as good as it once was, but they spoke French. Her first memory was how well Charles danced, but she could not remember that he died. John later sent her a copy of the letter with black borders that she had sent Sally at the time.

They mostly talked about her life. She told about her husband who had joined the French army in Algeria, was taken prisoner, escaped, and joined the Resistance. She

and her three children had gone to Provence after the
Germans had conquered France and occupied the north.
They had lived in Paris after the war, but her husband
had died of cancer a few years ago. One of her granddaughters was a student of English and wanted to teach
it someday. It was just a pleasant time. John asked her
if there were people still living who would have known
Charles or possibly even Sally, and she promised to give
him names and addresses. They took their leave with mutual promises to stay in touch and see each other. John
was thrilled to have established a tie with his mother and
the past.

He wrote the people whose names Katie sent him.
They were a handful because they would have had to
be in their eighties to have been young in the twenties.
Two old ladies replied that they remembered Charles
and had been friends of his mother. A retired architect,
Pierre Avenac, who had known Charles at the L'École
des Beaux-Arts and had been friends thereafter, responded that he had been very fond of Charles. A few
children, contemporaries of Julie and John, answered
that they did not remember or know about his family.
This was not surprising because the French do not
reach out to bring strangers into their family lives. A
promising letter came from M. Claude Picard, a bank
president, who had known Charles when they were
both young men about town and remembered Sally
as well. He had been a member of the same smart set

surrounding Katie. He wrote a very cordial letter inviting them to visit him in Paris or his country home in Normandy. The results accounted for all the letters that he had written.

Then they had a shock. An unsigned letter, written in English, arrived without a return address. It was written in bold letters: "If you know what is good for you, you will stay away and stop any attempt to dig up the past." It was a clear threat, but John could not let it go. He did not want to stop his search for the past just when it was bearing fruit. Julie did not agree: "You have learned what you wanted to know. You have waited too long to learn anything new. Stop it now." Of course she was right in the short run and perhaps in the long run, but John could not suppress his curiosity.

He told Katie about the letter and she was mystified. One day, when they three of them were having lunch, she remembered an event. Uncle Charles had worked in 1927 for a firm of architects and designers who both built and furnished houses. He advised on interiors and furnishings even after new owners had occupied their homes, most of which were quite grand. Katie remembered that there had been some jewel thefts from the new homes and that Charles's firm had been investigated. Was there a possible inside job in which jewel thieves were alerted by informants from the firm? All she could remember was that nothing ever happened and that Charles died the next year. This was a tantalizing story, but what to do with it? Were jewell thieves tracking John? It seemed absurd.

John wanted to do something but what? He told the story to a senior official at the Sorbonne who called a friend at the Surete and inquired what might be done. The friend arranged for John to call on an Inspector Henri Rambeau. John suspected that it was a courtesy call. The Inspector was rather elegant looking, with a well tailored suit and sharp gallic features. He was pleased with John's French, complimenting him on it. After John had told his story he thought for a moment

And then said there was little that could be done. The warning note had perhaps come from someone who had heard about John's explorations and did not want to be contacted should other old friends be turned up.

"We French are very private about family," he said. "It is not uncommon for us to invite people that we do not know well to entertain them by inviting them out to a restautrant rather than having them at home. I would not worry but I would advise you to leave well enough alone and limit yourself to the few people whom you have contacted."

John told him the story about the jewell robberies in 1927 and Rambeau remembered them because there were a series of thefts from those years that had not been solved. He sent for files and gave a John a 1927 newspaper clipping describing the thefts. One of the stories gave the name of the Paris detective who had investigated the case, an Inspector Henri Daimon. Rambeau had worked with Daimon before the old man retired.

"These thefts were very mysterious," Rambeau said. "They were clearly inside jobs. Someone had access to the houses as they were being furnished and learned where jewells were kept. Burglaries followed that were not often discovered because the thieves left no traces. The thefts might not be discovered until the lady of the house wished to wear the jewells. I can see why your uncle's firm was investigated but nothing was ever discovered."

John thanked Rambeau and went home but his curiosity was really piqied. The warning letter and Rambeau's story might fit together or they might not. He talked it over with Julie that night and suggested that he might like to talk with the old detective Henri Daimon, Julie was very skeptical. She was much more sensible than he was, which, aside from love, was one reason that he had married her. He also thought that she was smarter but did not tell her that so often. Still, he wanted to call Daimon and found his name in the telephone directory. He got Julie to agree to a visit only if she went with him so one day they went in search of a man who turned out to be a neighbor in the Marais. The old man had told John on telephone that he doubted that he could help him but would be happy to talk.

Daimon's apartment was comfortably furnished, and he was a comfortable man. He offered tea, coffee, sherry, wine, or whiskey as it was late afternoon. He was pleasantly plump with a shaggy mustache and disarming eyes. One could see how he might calm suspects before they knew what they might say. One could relax with him, if one were guilty of something, until it was too late. He had worked as a private detective for business firms after his retirement and said that his detecting antennae were still finally honed. He believed that the employees of Charles's firm were innocent but that a friend of an employee might have been able to get inside information about the houses through employees unbeknownst to them. Charles was a possibility because his work took him into the houses once they were built, furnished, and occupied. He never suspected Charles, whom he described as a naïve American, but wondered about his friends. Of course that was the point of departure. He remembered Charles well as "l'Americain qui était française." Charles wanted to be French and was blind to such an impossibility.

The old detective offered to look back into the history of jewel thefts and jewel thieves in Paris for any clues to the crimes that he had investigated. He warned that someone might feel threatened by any inquiry about Charles for what it might uncover about the firm. This was thin ice for John. He was not in the detective business, and the old boy was probably leading him on. But he bit the apple and asked Daimon to look into the past to see what he could find. He agreed not to look into the lives of any of Charles's friends.

Not long after that Julie and John met with two old friends of his mother for tea at Katie's in early October. The two ladies were quite grand. The Countess d'Argnac walked on the ground as if she owned it, but she was the soul of courtesy. They spoke French.

"Sally was such a sweet, happy American girl. We were all young and cheerful in those years. I was not a countess but a 'haute bourgeoisie' like Katie, with no idea what my life would be like. Even so, Sally was different. We took Paris and its pleasures for granted. But she was in a state of wonder about the city and its charms. We were young and hopeful but also realistic about people and the pit-falls of life and how people might disappoint one, but not Sally. She was so thoroughly American, which was one reason we loved her."

The Countess had married into a rich family, but it was a poor marriage. Fortunately for her, the Count had been killed early in the war. He had joined his regiment and fallen as the Germans swept into France. She had left Paris for his estate in Brittany and lived quietly with her children during the German occupation. On returning to Paris she married a prosperous attorney and resumed her former life. She was still a Countess in her own eyes, even though her first husband's brother took the title and the estate and his wife presumed to become the Countess. So there were two countesses. Not that anyone minded because the origins of the titles were buried in history and had no legal significance.

Marie Beauvais, the other friend, had been a concert violinist in her day, not as a solo performer, but as member of prominent string quartets. Her career had been delayed by the war because she had left Paris for the country. She had never married, but one suspected that she had enjoyed lovers because at eighty she was strikingly handsome with snow white hair, an arched French nose, and high cheekbones. Both women were so very French in that beneath their genuine cordiality there was a cutting edge that could not be defined. It was perhaps an absence of sentimentality. They both remembered his mother quite well. They liked the openness and friendliness that make the French like Americans in contrast to the English. They told stories about playing hide-and-seek in a large country house at night and attending parties and picnics and balls. They recalled that Charles would not join Sally at concerts or the opera unless they sat in the most expensive seats. She was on a tight allowance from her father, but he had Aunt Gladys's legacy.

Neither of them had a clue about the threatening letter, nor did they take it too seriously. French privacy about family was a reality. John and Julie enjoyed both women, although, as with Katie, a few anecdotes from memory cannot recapture the past. He wanted a time machine with which to see Sally and Charles. Eventually he found that their letters home best captured their lives, at least as they saw themselves.

Julie and John took leave of the ladies and went to

see M. Pierre Avenac, Charles's friend from L'École des Beaux-Arts. He lived in a Left Bank neighborhood settled by artists, actors, writers, and intellectuals of all stripes. He was round, with a oval, smiling face and an expanse of stomach that betrayed good living. His apartment was draped with paintings, photographs of buildings and churches, and portraits of attractive women.

"Oh, Charleee. He was so innocent. Such a sweet boy. He found a 'mother,' an older woman who encouraged and looked after him, especially after his aunt died. He called her 'Tata.' I was never sure of her name. She helped him understand Parisian society, guided him in social encounters, and looked after him. She was attractive and middle aged and I was never sure whether they enjoyed the bedroom together, but it could have been," he said, laughing.

He dismissed the jewel theft business as police foolishness.

"Charles never saw any jewels. Valuable jewels were locked up, and the police were grasping at straws. We had a wonderful time as young men about town. I loved Sally and her American roommates, "les femmes américaines." They were surely captive to his charms as well. He was not a romantic lover kind of Frenchman but an entertainer and charmer like Maurice Chevalier. He had finally married, he said, a woman as entertaining and enjoyable as himself. She had "départé" a few years ago, but he was consoling himself with widows and other available ladies.

He had no children, but his life was filled with "les amis, les femmes, et le bon appétit."

They left him with regret and hopes of seeing him again for no particular reason except enjoyment. Two weeks later they called on M. Claude Picard, the financier, in the rich 17th Arrondissement. His house was right on the street, a large stone structure surely designed to impress the visitor during the second empire of Napoleon II, a regime for the rich. A butler welcomed them and led them through a grand hallway to a staircase up to a richly furnished drawing room on the second floor where M. Picard was waiting. He was a tall man with a long face and a full head of black hair. The face was severe, but the smile and bow were welcoming. He spoke English beautifully.

"I am so happy to see you. Charles was my friend when we were both young and irresponsible. Oh, such plaisirs we had. I was the third son of a count. He had a social position but little money. So I had to find a way to survive in the world. A kind relative loaned me some money so that I might buy my way into the bank that I now head, but it was luck that my relation would help.

"Charles and I enjoyed each other, but we were very different. He was an aesthete who enjoyed social and artistic life for the enjoyment they gave. He liked glamorous people, which fitted him for his work because he helped them design their homes. I was more practical, wishing to use my social position to advance myself, and I have done so throughout my career. A banker must build his fortune on his connections."

M. Picard was an investment banker, and his bank, as they eventually learned, was particularly active in former French colonies in North Africa, Syria, and Indochina. His daughter, Lily, and his son-in-law, Paul de Frontenac, worked in the bank as well. His son, Marc, was an archeologist, based in a large museum in Paris. Marc,a bachelor, spent much of his time in field work in North Africa, Syria, Iraq, and Egypt.

Picard was a widower, his wife having died in 1955. He had not remarried. John and Julie had the general impression that his bank was his life. He told them that he traveled extensively on bank business and also visited the digs of his son where he had learned archeology and met a number of patrons of archeology. Marc's museum supported him and his work financially, but his projects were expensive and he found patrons in France and in countries where he was working. Rich provincials in North Africa, for example, wished to provide support for excavations into past glories. M. Picard invited John and Julie back to meet his daughter and her husband, and they promised to keep in touch.

They stopped by to see Katie later just to visit. She had remembered a long-lost friend of Charles, a Hungarian aristocrat named Andrés Molnar. He seemed to have no special purpose to his life except enjoying high society, along with Charles. Much to the surprise of people who knew him, he left Paris in 1928 and had not been heard from since. He was from a family of ancient Hungarian aristocrats with a large country estate. Katie said that she had remembered his name because he had been interviewed by police during the jewel thief business. She wondered what had happened to him and his family during and after the war. She could not imagine that the threatening letter was in any way related to him, but it had still come into her mind.

When John back to the Sorbonne, he asked colleagues if there was a scholar of modern Hungary at the university and was told that he should talk with Professor Ferenc Nagy. He called Nagy and they had lunch a few days later. Nagy was a Hungarian but long time resident of Paris and the Sorbonne faculty since the 1930's. He was both portly and courtly with a kind face . He was very much interested in John's story and responded at some length.

"Molnar was a younger son of an old aristocratic family who did live in Paris in the twenties for a few years, but he could not support himself and returned to Hungary. His family had a large estate near Budapest, which was managed by his older brother, Count Gyorgy. He could have stayed on the estate but chose to work for the government in Budapest for Admiral Horthy, who was the Regent Leader of the nation in the absence of a king. His family was evidently close to Horthy, who had been the head of the Austro-Hungarian navy in World War One. Horthy's government was benignly authoritarian and was supported by aristocrats and peasants rather than the professional and commercial classes, who were more liberal in their politics.

"Horthy tried to keep his distance from Hitler, for example, refusing to let German troops cross Hungary as they invaded Russia. Hungary was a nation dominated by aristocrats, a modern feudal system, with strong sanction from the Catholic Church. A Nazi regime would have threatened such institutions and traditions. Horthy gave lip service to Hitler but held back in numerous ways. Yet German pressure pushed Hungarian legislatures to pass increasingly severe anti-Jewish laws. The right-wing Arrow Cross movement and party were active in anti-Jewish activities, and male Jews were confined in what came to resemble concentration camps. Many of them were deported to Poland under the supervision of Adolf Eichmann. Toward the end of the war when German defeat became clear, Horthy put out feelers to the Allies, and although he was briefly imprisoned after peace came, he was released and moved to Portugal where he lived out the rest of his life.

"Your man Molnar was an aide to Horthy throughout the war. We know his position more than we know what he did. There were reports that he was involved in the deportation of Jews, but nothing was ever proved and he 'escaped,' if that is the word, to Portugal and died there at some time, leaving a wife and two sons about whom nothing is known."

They discussed the possibility that one of Molnar's

sons might be in Paris and learned of the letter to Charles's friends. They would surely not wish to discuss their father's career with John or anyone else. John let it drop, but stored it away in his mind for future questions should they arise.

After this entire story was over, and John and Julie had returned to America, John looked in Charles's letters from France to his Uncle Albert, then living in Strasbourg in 1927, and found an account of a visit to Hungary in the autumn of that year. Sally had come to France in July and in August, and they embarked on a grand European tour, which took them first to Vienna and then to Budapest. An excerpt from the letter read:

> "We left for another delightful place, that of the Count Szechlengi, where we stayed for a week. There we met the governor Regent of Hungary, for it's still a kingdom. He was quite a nice man, and his wife was rather pretty. He was formerly Admiral Horthy. They were living in the summer Royal Residence, his favorite place. . . . The Hungarians are so loyal to their king, and it is only because of politics that he is not in Hungary. It is only a question of a few years when he will be back."

John had no way to connect the meeting with Horthy

with Charles's friend in Paris, Andrés Molnar, but there may have been a connection. Not long after that, Molnar left France for Hungary and went to work for Horthy. The letter revealed that Charles had swallowed the royalist loyalty to the king of Hungary so typical of the old aristocratic families. Charles was a snob and politically naïve.

Nothing much happened in this story during the rest of the autumn months. They kept in touch with Katie but saw nothing of the others in Paris. There was no word from Daimon. To their astonishment in November they received a telephone call out of the blue from Katie telling them that Claude Picard had been murdered in the library of his home in Paris. Someone had bashed him in the head with a heavy bookend. There was no evidence of breaking and entering. Nothing was stolen.

Chapter 2

Not long after the murder John Page received a call from Inspector Jules Lavin of the Paris police. Lavin knew only that they had visited Picard, presumably from Picard's daughter, and asked him about his acquaintance with the French banker. John told him the basic story about wanting to meet friends of his mother and uncle and mentioned the warning letter. Lavin asked if he could come to their apartment to to talk with them, and of course, they agreed. It was a cold, wet November day and Lavin was happy to sit in their warm living room by the fire with a cup of tea. He was tall and lanky with a long face and clever eyes that seemed to take in everything. Julie noticed him scanning their book titles and family pictures as if he were Sherlock Holmes about to tell them about their lives.

John told his story in fuller detail including his talk

wth Daimon. He expressed embarrassment at playing private detective. Lavin murmured quiet disapproval but said that he knew Daimon, respected him, and would talk with him. Then he described the murder scene.

"Picard was lying by his desk in his library. The killer struck with a heavy bookend that was on his desk. He was evidently killed by one very forceful blow, according to the wound. This may have been a sudden and abrupt action by the killer that was not planned. He reached for the first weapon at hand. Picard may have known his killer, or at least he admitted him to his house because there was no evidence of forced entry. It was the butler's night off, and none of the small staff of kitchen servants or maids was in the house. Picard lived alone except for the small house staff. There was one peculiarity. The police received a call that they should send an ambulance to Picard's house. He was dead when found by the ambulance attendants and the police. The doctor at the scene thought that the blow had killed Picard but said that, though unconscious, he might have lived for a few minutes after the blow. This suggests that the killer knew Picard and had qualms, but the person was not willing to confess."

Next he told them an unexpected story that Picard's bank was under investigation for financial irregularities. The Ministry of Finance was in charge, but it could become a police matter for his knowledge, if not his authority. He spoke in confidence but said that the murder would probably prompt him to look into the banker's money matters. Lavin did not seem to suspect John of anything, although one cannot be sure, but he talked as if they were allies in the work to come.

Lavin had several leads to pursue. The financial problems of the bank required inquiry. The lives of Picard's daughter, son, and son-in-law were necessarily part of any investigation. Picard's private life, friends, and activities had to be explored. Lavin decided that he would ask where and how Picard found the funds to invest in the bank. His public story had always been that a gift from a relative to a poor relation, himself, had made the difference. The relative had never been identified, even to Picard's daughter. She had been told that a distant cousin had helped him without the need for repayment. The gift was a legacy rather than a loan. Lavin decided that it should be possible to document any such gift from the banker's personal financial records.

He also talked with retired Inspector Henri Daimon, whom he had known when he was a young detective. Lavin wanted to know about a possible association of Picard with Andrés Molnar, the Hungarian playboy, at the time of the jewel thefts. The old man was happy to be back in harness if only temporarily. They set about to explore Picard's past finances. John had instructed Daimon to leave Picard alone for fear of informing the author of the warning letter. However, the letter was now evidence in a murder investigation.

Daimon had explored the police files of the original
robberies. Suspicion was cast on Charles's firm because
the thefts had occurred in houses served by the firm.
They were not the only jewel thefts in Paris at that time,
but correspondence of the thefts with the contracts and
assignments of the design house was clear. The police
had interviewed every member of the firm from president to porters, but uncovered nothing. The thefts took
the form of subtle burglaries in which thieves entered
the houses when no one was home and carried off jewels
without evidence that anything was missing. Discoveries
lagged behind the actual thefts, or so it was thought. The
firm began to suffer loss of business when the pattern
became clear to clients quite apart from the police work.
Then the robberies stopped as abruptly as they had begun. The police assumed that the thieves had decided to
quit while they were ahead of any detection. Nothing was
ever uncovered. It had not been possible to investigate
the friends of every employee, but some inquiries were
quietly pursued. Charles had such wide social connections that they could not be fully explored. Most of his
friends were well to do, especially those with aristocratic
names. Two friends of slender means were Claude Picard
and Andrés Molnar, and the police had interviewed both.
Not much could be learned about Molnar because he
left France for Hungary not long after Charles died. This
looked suspicious to the police at the time, but there was
no evidence beyond personal friendship. An inside job

would require not only an informant but also professional jewel thieves and their organization and methods. The police had a good knowledge of such people, but it could not be connected to any suspects.

Lavin and Daimon decided to take a fresh look into the source of Picard's money that enabled him to buy into the bank. They looked into his personal bank accounts in 1927, the year that he joined the bank as a junior officer. The bank had such records, but they were incomplete for any other financial records that he might have had. The bank's records did reveal a substantial investment in the bank by Picard and his subsequent appointment to the firm as an officer. He was an investor in the bank and a potential partner in the firm. There was one fact that aroused their interest. In 1927 the bank received a very large deposit of funds from a secret Swiss bank account that was directed to Picard as the beneficiary. Picard had explained to the bank officer that it was a gift from a relative, and the bank had accepted his story.

After mulling the matter over for a time, the two detectives had a fresh idea. Why not see if Picard had any relatives in 1927 who might have given him a boost in life?

Lavin asked Katie for any knowledge that she might have of Picard relatives and kept John and Julie informed of his search in case they should discover anything new about Picard's history. But nothing was forthcoming. Demographic data in public archives might give an answer. Picard was the third son of an aristocratic family that enjoyed status but lacked a fortune. His father lived a modest life in a country house on a small inheritance, and his mother had no independent wealth. His two older brothers had each gone his own way. One was a lawyer who had been in Paris during the war but had immigrated to Canada in the 1950s and was practicing law in Montreal. The other was a retired army officer who served in World Wat Two, and the French colonial wars in Indochina and Algeria. Their father was the first and only son of a man similar to himself, a country squire. Their mother's family were solid middle class without social pretensions. There was no trace of an affluent cousin, aunts, or uncles, or of an extended family. That cast some doubt on Picard's story about a legacy of a rich, benevolent relative.

In the meantime Daimon had discovered that some organizations of jewel thieves in Marseille had invested their profits in money laundering, smuggling, and other worthy enterprises. Some of these thieves had been caught and their rings partially dismantled through criminal convictions over a period of years, stretching from prewar time to the present. These organizations had also invested, much like the Mafia, in legitimate businesses as a front for the laundering of profits. This story could help explain Picard's money and a source of the funds from the Swiss bank if he had been an accomplice of the jewel thieves linked to Charles's fashion house.

John Page's only connection with this story and

murder was the threatening note that he received. Lavin asked whether there might be a connection between his approach to Picard and the man's murder, as if inquiry into Picard's history might uncover a story from his past that someone wished to conceal. The mysterious deposit from the Swiss bank in 1927 may have been related in some way.

Lavin's next line of inquiry was to interview Picard's two children, Lily and Marc, and his son-in-law, Paul. Marc Picard had come from near Tangier in Morocco for his father's funeral and intended to go back to his dig as soon as possible because it was his project and time was important. He was almost fifty, a well-known archeologist, who specialized in uncovering lost cities. Lavin found him to be open and intelligent but without any sense of why his father might have been killed. He knew only in a general way that the bank was having financial problems. His income came from his salary at the archeological department of his museum as well as research foundations and gifts from wealthy friends of archeology at home and abroad. He was a bachelor, once married but long divorced, and without children.

"Surely this was a bungled burglary," he asked Lavin. "My father must have surprised the thieves, and they panicked and killed him impulsively."

Lavin agreed that was a possibility but nothing was taken, and there were many valuable items in the house: paintings, silver, china, and crystal. Why would professional thieves, surprised or not, pass up taking something? He was not entirely convinced by his own argument. Burglars were not usually murderers, but they could have struck Picard to stop his protests and then panicked because they were not killers. But a murder had taken place, and it was his duty to find the killer or killers. A grapevine network was set by the police to inquire among the community of Paris criminals about a crime of violence in a burglary, but nothing surfaced after two weeks.

Marc Picard told Lavin that he would return to Morocco after the funeral but would be available if needed for any reason. He also mentioned that friends in a bank in Tangier were interested in investing in his father's bank and that discussions had been initiated and were ongoing. The bank's foundation also helped support his current research project. The officers of the Tangier bank were French and Spanish and very familiar with European banking. So Marc went off, and Lavin turned his attention to Lily and her husband.

John and Julie Page had attended Picard's funeral and, quite by chance, Julie recognized Marc Picard whom she had met at a professional meeting in New York not long before. They also met Picard's daughter and her husband at the same time and enjoyed exchanging stories of the lives of their seniors in the nineteen twenties.

Both Lily and Paul de Frontenac worked in the bank, she in public relations and he in investments. Lavin interviewed them separately. Lily was forty-five, a striking woman with coal black hair and black eyes. She had been a journalist with *Le Figaro*, a conservative paper, covering economics and public affairs, but had joined the bank ten years before at the request of her father. She was the director of publicity and public relations. She could not believe that anyone would want to kill her father. According to her he had few close friends and a very limited social life. He ran the bank with a strong executive hand with the assistance of two loyal lieutenants of long tenure. She had to admit that if the bank was in some financial difficulty, he was surely responsible, but this did not match her picture of him as a hard-nosed, sensible man.

After this conversation with Lavin, she paused, as if she had more to say, and then stopped talking. Lavin asked if she had anything to add, and she paused again. He waited, and after an awkward moment, she began to talk.

"There is one fact that you might need to know about my father. He had a longtime mistress after my mother died in 1955. Her name was Anne Beauvais. I was seventeen when mother died, and my brother was nineteen. My father was a good parent, and we finished our educations with his encouragement. I am not sure when he made the liaison with Anne, but it was in the late 1950s. We met her a few times and I rather liked her, but I never knew her well. She had been an actress under the name of Camille Lucet. My father did not bring her into our family life nor did he take her into public more than a few times. She lived in the country in a house that he owned and maintained. She had never been married to my knowledge. My general impression is that she was a warm, empathetic person who had been a stage actress but retired when the relationship began. She perhaps gave my father the affection he needed. He told us of her death without details nor did he display any grief, and yet his mood was bleak for some months.

"There is more to the story. They had a son who is our half brother. Neither Paul nor I ever met him, nor did Father ever mention him, but Anne did on one or two occasions. He had taken her last name, Lucet. She made it clear that he was Father's son, perhaps because she wanted us to know that he was a blood relative, and maybe because of any future inheritance he might have received. However, my father never acknowledged that the son existed nor, to my knowledge, did he do anything to help him financially. He must have supported the son as he provided for the mother, but I know nothing beyond that. I would have hoped that my father was more generous than that, but he was very tight about money and business. He grew up poor but with high social standing, and the disparity rankled him, certainly as a young man, and despite his money, it stayed with him throughout his life."

Lavin was fascinated by this story and decided that

he must find records of the mother and son. Research uncovered Anne's birth and death. She was born in the Auvergne in 1925 and died in Paris in 1986. She had lived in a country town in Normandy. Her son, Jean Lucet, was born in 1960 in a Paris hospital. The records for country residence revealed that Jean went to school as a boy and to the local Lycée. After that the record was blank. Lavin could find no trace of him in any national records. He seemed to have vanished from the earth or, at least, from France.

Anne's birth records revealed that she had an older brother and a younger sister, born in the same town. It took some work to trace their adult lives. Lavin set his demographers to work, and they produced results because the French have excellent national records and are also proficient with numbers. The brother was Gilles Beauvais, a professional actor with a wide and varied career. He often acted with the Comédie-Française and a number of other companies. Lavin did not know him by his professional reputation because there were so many good professional actors in France. He was currently acting in a play in London. Anne's sister was Marie Beauvais, a well-known professional violinist who played with ensembles, especially string quartets, rather than as a solo artist. This woman was Katie's friend, whom John and Julie had met in Katie's home early in this adventure, but Lavin did not know this at the time that he found her.

Lavin talked with Marie and learned of the connection

with John Page, which was of interest to him because of the threatening letter that John had received. His greater interest was in finding Jean Lucet, but she was of no help. Her sister, Anne, had been an actress, and she had continued to act, using the stage name of Camille Lucet during the early years of her liaison with Picard, but eventually retired. She had given her son her stage name. Illness in the last years of her life had hampered her career. Marie had known Jean from his early childhood and had known that Picard was his father. She also knew Picard socially but not as well as Katie or the Countess. She remembered that Jean had been very intelligent and ambitious. Anne had great hopes for him despite his lack of social background. His mother died just as he was finishing his education at the local Lycée and planning to go to university. Marie knew that his father, Claude Picard, had supported him to that point and she knew that the relationship of father and son was distant, but she could say no more than that. And then Jean suddenly disappeared. For some years she had tried to find him without success. They had been close as aunt and nephew, and she was at a loss to understand his disappearance and his failure to contact her. Surely if he were in Paris she would see or hear of him, but nothing happened. She said that her brother had the same experience.

Lavin went to London to talk with Gilles Beauvais, the actor uncle, who was acting in a play on the London stage. They sat down in the restaurant of a hotel frequented by theater people and talked over lunch.

"Claude was devoted to Anne and looked after the boy generously as long as he was at home with Anne. He made no effort to get close to Jean or to learn anything much about him. I think that the boy felt this keenly. He wanted a father rather than a caretaker and complained to me about it. His mother felt this as well, but she cared for Picard and was also financially dependent on him, especially after she became ill and lost her income from acting, which was never great. I felt that the son surely suffered emotionally from his illegitimacy. It was obvious to all who knew him that he had no father. Only close friends knew that Picard was his father. He was also handicapped because he had no family name. A good name, even without money, is crucial to getting up and ahead in French society. Snobbery is greater than in England, even though the social distinctions are less visible. Of course he had no money unless Picard was going to help him. I never knew about this one way or the other. When he disappeared, I assumed that Picard had not offered to help him. From what I knew of the boy he would not have been content with a petit bourgeois career. He was ambitious and would not have settled for anything but a good life at the top."

He had never heard from Jean, even though they had been close. The whole thing was a mystery to his sister and him. They had not undertaken an elaborate search or paid someone to do it. They had assumed that he did not want to be found, for reasons of his own. They were also worried that he might have died or that a disaster might have harmed him, but what could they do? It was a profound puzzle to them.

Lavin was skeptical of their stories as too pat and too similar. If they had really been close to the boy, he or they surely would have kept in touch. Jean had no one else in the world other than them, and his actual relationship with his father was not known apart from these two reports. When he discussed his conversations with Daimon, the other detective got a strange expression on his face.

"I know someone who may know them well. Let me ask a question or two." The "someone" was Daimon's friend and onetime lover, Patti Roquet. She had been a torch singer and chanteuse, who was younger than Daimon and still sang in nightclubs on occasion. She did know Marie and Gilles Beauvais from the theater world.

Lavin called on her and found a most enjoyable lady. She was still very good looking in her sixties and was funny and seemingly carefree, like Daimon himself. They were close and saw each other regularly. More important, she had known Anne Beauvais, Picard's mistress, and knew of the son although she had never met him. She was also skeptical of Gilles's and Marie's stories. They had been close to the nephew, and he to them. They were affectionate people, and it was unlikely that he would disappear without their knowing where he was and what he was doing. She assumed they might be protecting him from something or someone. Lavin was not surprised by her comment and was uncertain what to do.

Chapter 3

Lavin resolved to keep looking for Jean but had to follow other leads for the time being. His colleagues at the Ministry of Finance gave him a clear picture of the Picard banks finances. It was undercapitalized and in debt because of investment losses. The bank had recommended financial offerings that had failed and hurt its customers as well as cut its profits. The Ministry was investigating, the question being whether the advice given shareholders was simply ill advised from hubris about the economy or fraudulent by pushing unreliable securities. The bank had initially made much money from purchases of its products. However, the chickens had come home to roost, and the bank was in trouble.

The gap between earnings and debt could possibly be made up by future investments in the bank. The number of partnerships would not have to grow. New investors could be limited partners without voting power on the board, controlled by the family, but the authority of the full partners would be diminished. If new investors claimed partnerships, control of the bank would change. The problems that the bank had created for itself were clearly the work of Claude Picard and his two partners. It was not quite the same as the problems faced by large banks in which experts would use complex and even esoteric financial formulae to estimate the risk of given investments. Such analysis depended upon projections on future economic conditions for their validity. Subjective hubris would lead to financial disaster if economic conditions changed for the worse. But officers at the top of the big banks might not understand the instruments they were selling. This was less likely with the Picard bank. Lavin was in touch with the regulators on this score. Picard's bank had engaged in such overconfident measures from the decisions of the three partners and a few associates, such as Paul de Frontenac. The difficulties could not be blamed on experts in the basement.

There were two other full partners, both of whom were longtime associates of Picard. The question for Lavin was whether they were associates or lieutenants. Lavin interviewed them and decided that they were lieutenants. Paul Louvois and Charles Bonnard were mature men, younger than Picard, whom he had brought into the bank. They paid for their investments and partnerships themselves, but neither was as enterprising as their master. He was the chief executive and the source of ideas. They had been implementers. They were loyal to Picard but had not been personal friends. They both knew of his relationship with Anne but only in the vaguest way, or so they said. Neither of them had ever met her, nor did they know anything about a son. They were defensive about the financial losses of the bank and were not willing to blame their chief, blaming the troubles on the collapse of world markets in 1987 that damaged sales and expectations. They were busy soliciting new investments but were at sea as to who would run the bank in the immediate future as well as long term. Neither aspired to the job; they did not feel quite up to it. Both suggested that Paul de Frontenac was the likely successor. Lily was the heir to Picard's estate and his controlling ownership of the bank. Neither of them mentioned her as a possible successor. Bonnard told Lavin,

"We were surely imprudent in our investments and financial offerings in the last few years but we were banking on continued prosperity and the economic downturn in 1987 caught us short with debts that exceeded our income. We will catch up as times improve. Paul de Frontenac is a very sensible man who could not always control his father in law. Picard was very bold and imaginative and also very stubborn. He did not like to be challenged. The two of us got along with him by being loyal lieutenants who never challenged him."

Lavin filed this characterization of the murdered man

away in his mind as a possible clue as to what might have happened in his study the night that he was killed.

Lily assumed the presidency of the firm, much to the surprise of the two vice presidents and financial circles. She had been an economic journalist who was also well acquainted with government, including important people in high places. Her husband became a vice president, a new position, and it appeared to outsiders that they would establish a working partnership. Lavin thought it possible that Lily Picard, and perhaps her husband, could have planned her father's murder in order to take control of the bank. But it seemed unlikely. De Frontenac was already in a high position and Lily would inherit control when her father died. He was not sure how to uncover evidence of any such plot so let the matter rest for the moment.

The situation left Lavin without clues about motives for Picard's murder. He needed to look further into the murdered man's private life but first turned to colleagues in the Ministry of Finance who were investigating the bank's financial history for fraud. If the bank had financial problems, was there a reason that anyone might want Picard removed from the scene? This could have perhaps been done more easily through financial means, such as buying him out or government prosecution on criminal charges. The latter course was unlikely. The government had replaced no executives in troubled banks. It could buy the bank outright as much of the banking sector was already publicly owned. But there had been no such discussion before Picard was killed. If new investors wanted to remove him, they could do it with enough money.

Lavin thought of other possibilities and returned, in his mind, to Henri Daimon's report of diversification of the money of jewel thieves into legitimate business enterprises. Threats to such enterprises might lead to protective actions. Picard had not explained the source of his original ability to invest in the bank. More investigation into his past and private life was necessary. Paul de Frontenac was in charge of examining potential investors in the bank. New shares might be created but not in sufficient number to dislodge Lily's control. She had to find fresh funds to strengthen the bank's assets to ensure her control. Her leverage was guaranteed in that new investors would be given no voting power on the board that she controlled. The corporate charter guaranteed that. The only way to gain control of the firm away from Lily was to buy her out, and she was not selling. Shares were not on a stock market. The bank did require fresh funds, however, and new investors might bargain with Lily about their role in the governance of the bank. Nothing of that kind had yet emerged.

Lavin pursued his questions through the Ministry of Finance official who was inquiring into the bank's recent financial history. Eduard Bonoir was an accomplished sleuth into bank financial histories. He told Lavin that he saw hubris and greed as the reasons for the bank's failures. It was not unique among French and European banks in this regard. He was interested in suitor investors to assess their capabilities for righting the ship. A Spanish bank had recently come to his attention. It was represented in France by two brothers who were doing the bargaining with de Frontenac. They were Spanish, Carlos and Juan Ramirez. The Spanish bank proposed to invest a large sum of money in the bank but wanted a full partnership with a share in management. Neither Lily nor her husband was willing to do that so negotiations had stalled. A foreign bank could easily buy a non-voting membership, and the money would certainly be influential in the bank's policies. Lily wanted to control the bank without full partners. Yet she needed money so her husband looked for other investors as he bargained with the Spanish brothers.

Paul de Frontenac had then stepped up the negotiations with a bank in Tangier, which was seeking investment rather than partnership. Representatives of the bank would have to visit Paris and get their own experts to examine the bank's books before making an offer. Lily had passed information about the Spanish and Moroccan possibilities to Bonoir of the Ministry of Finance, and he informed Inspector Lavin in turn.

For lack of any strong leads Lavin decided to ask Bonoir to look for anything untoward in his inquiry into the finances of the two potential investors and the official agreed to pursue the matter. The studies took time

so Lavin thought of exploring the histories of the two
Spanish brothers. They had lived in France for some years
as agents of the Spanish bank. Their headquarters were in
Marseilles. Their chief responsibility was to invest funds
in French enterprises. That seemed legitimate to Lavin,
but one matter gave him pause. The brothers were citizens of Spain, but they had been born in Portugal in the
late 1940s. Their mother was Spanish, and they had taken
her last name for business and professional purposes,
which was customary. Their father's name was Andrés
Molnar, the elusive Hungarian who had been the friend
of John's uncle in the 1920s and a lieutenant of Admiral
Horthy, the Hungarian wartime dictator. This fact, by
itself, was a historical coincidence, but Lavin thought that
he would follow it up because their father's past was a bit
shady. For that he would need to know more about their
bank, and he relied on M. Bonoir. Such research was not
easy because the Spanish bank records in general were
privileged by law, especially to foreign inquiries, and the
Spanish bank was not a commercial entity but a privately
owned investment firm. The owners were a Spanish family, not unlike the French Picard family. The firm had in
recent years acquired ownership in banks in Gibraltar,
Mexico, and Buenos Aires. The bank had also reached
out to banks in London but without results to date. The
president of the firm and the head of the family was
Alfred Cruz. Bonoir reported that the bank was seemingly loaded with cash and ambitious in its conquests.

There was a past connection with Andrés Molnar, the father of the brothers. He had made large deposits in the bank after he took up residence in Portugal. No one knew where he had gotten that money.

Lavin remembered that Molnar had been in Paris in 1927 during the investigation of the jewel thefts. Nothing had been discovered, but he had left France for Hungary not long afterward. At this point Lavin went back to his old colleague Henri Daimon who had investigated the original crimes and had been following the fortunes of jewel thieves, past and present, by agreement with Lavin. Daimon had found a record of money laundering by Marseille jewel thieves, but there was no evidence to tie Molnar to any such past activity except the possibility of his connection with the thefts in 1927. This was all very circumstantial, and Lavin was grounded in speculation until a dramatic event occurred. An attempt was made to kill Lily de Frontenac.

Lily was standing on her garden terrace one late October evening. It was not quite dark, and she remembered that she could see and enjoy the red poppies in her garden when a shot just missed her. She kept her self-possession and quickly dropped to the paving stones behind an iron chair. There were no more shots. She was able to crawl to a large bush, get behind it, and then crawl around a corner to the other side of the house and through a French door into a room. Her husband was not at home, and the staff, who were elsewhere in the house, did not hear anything. She immediately called the police. Inspector Lavin was alerted and came within short notice. He darkened the house and stood on the terrace trying to estimate the direction from which the shot might have come. The de Frontenac home was surrounded by homes of similar size, all with back or side terraces. The shot could have come from any one of them. A police canvass of the neighboring houses revealed nothing from the inhabitants except that two families were not at home. It would have been easy to enter a terrace through a side yard, fire a shot, and slip away unseen.

Lavin concluded that someone wished to remove Lily not only from life but perhaps more important from the presidency of the bank. This conclusion stimulated his speculations. It seemed unlikely that the Spanish bank as an organization would resort to such violence for economic purposes. Was it possible that investors in the bank, anxious for action, might have acted rashly? An answer to this question would require a more thorough look at the bank but one beyond the goals of the Ministry of Finance. They were interested in Lily de Frontenac's bank and its resources and could not go beyond that point. Lavin and Daimon had to think of something else.

Chapter 4

Daimon was well acquainted with the criminal class in the business of stealing jewels, and he had to find an informant who might be of use to them. One woman came to mind. In the past he had known a woman married to an accomplished thief. She was never charged or convicted of a crime, but Daimon was well aware that she knew the ins and outs of thievery through her husband, Guillame Carbonet. Simone Carbonet never divorced her husband, even though he went to prison for ten years in 1940. Unfortunately he died after seven years, dashing their expectations of future, postwar prosperity. Her husband's colleagues in crime had stopped supporting her financially at that point. There had been no word of her in police or criminal circles since that time. Daimon had met her several times and rather liked her. She was an opportunist rather than a professional criminal, who was happy to live off her husband's "earnings." *Amorality* was the appropriate term rather than *immorality*. Daimon had to answer several questions: How could he find her? What would he ask her to do? Why would she agree? What inducements could he offer?

They discovered that she was living quietly in a suburb of Paris. She was then about seventy-five. Who was to approach her and with what inducements? No one but Daimon could do it. He was not the man who put her husband in jail. That was a colleague now dead. Did she know anything about contemporary crime? Why would she cooperate with Daimon? She could simply deny knowledge. She had no reason to help the Picard family. After some thought, Daimon had an inspiration. Simone was Jewish. She might have a strong reason to get even with Andrés Molnar if he had been involved with deporting Jews to death camps in Eastern Europe. She might have no love for his sons either if they were his heirs.

Her file disclosed that the organization of thieves of which Guillame was a senior partner supported her while he was in prison, perhaps in anticipation of income when he was freed. However, after he died, they cut her off cold, without a centime. Her mother helped until her two children, a boy and a girl, could meet her needs. Daimon took the direct approached. He called her on the telephone, introduced himself and asked if she were willing to talk with him about a case long past in which she might be helpful The answer was yes, with some hesitation. She would meet him on a designated bench in the Jardin du Luxembourg on a given day.

He went to the agreed location on a beautiful, sunny day and waited. In due time a tall, slender woman walked up and asked if he were M. Daimon. She then sat on the bench and looked at him carefully. Her face had high cheekbones and a firm jaw with few wrinkles. Her voice was low with some melody. She quietly asked him what he wanted of her. He very carefully told her that he was looking into the life and finances of Andrés Molnar. She did not respond, but he could tell by her eyes that she recognized the name. He added that he was working on a case in which it was important to learn the source of Molnar's money when he went to live in Portugal after the war. He then told her of Molnar's wartime record in the deportation of Jews from Hungary to Poland and the Ukraine. She seemed not to know this but showed great interest. He finally said that he wanted to know if Molnar had had some past relationship with jewel thieves and their laundering of money into business enterprises. It was important, he said, because it would explain matters in a case on which he was working.

She listened carefully and paused a while before replying. She knew nothing about Molnar's wartime activities. She knew his name because it was common knowledge among rings of jewel thieves. She knew nothing of the 1927 robberies, it would not surprise her if Molnar had been involved.

"He was a gentleman thief who kept his hands clean

by working through professional thieves. He would often identify the work to be done and rely on them to do the actual burglaries.

"I did not know about his life in Hungary during the war but am not surprised. He seems to have escaped any charges of complicity then as well"

Lavin believed that she was telling him the truth, thanked her, and promised not to tell anyone that they had talked. They said good-bye and parted. He was grateful for a confirmation what was known about Molnar. Still detecting was an incremental business much of the time. There was no evidence that any laundered money had been invested in the Spanish bank or any reason for such investors to wish to kill Lily de Frontenac. Someone did wish to kill her, presumably to eliminate her from the leadership of the bank, but who could that be?

Lavin and Daimon put their heads together and decided that they needed help from the French Foreign Office, particularly its Office of Intelligence. There might be information about Molnar that the office would not necessarily have shared with the police. They could have been interested in his political background to the exclusion of anything else. Lavin had to go to the Chief Inspector of Police for permission to talk with the Foreign Office. This was especially the case because his query was not directly about a crime and seemed to intrude into foreign affairs.

This took some persuading. M. Paul Martain sat behind his broad desk, which was clean of all clutter except the transparent glass pyramid he had won for distinction as a police officer. His office was equally free of clutter with its thick carpet and rich traditional décor. He was an aristocrat in bearing, if not in birth, because he was a mandarin, a graduate of one of the Grandes Ecoles in Paris from which most French high-ranking civil servants, top businessmen, and most of the prominent politicians emerged. He was a graduate of the National College of Administration. This was not uncommon among the higher ranks of the Sûreté, but for the most part, the police bureaucracy consisted of men who had begun walking a beat and had worked their way up through the ranks. This was one reason that they were good policemen. They knew crime from its grass roots. This was Lavin's background. He was not even a Parisian; he began his career in Lyon. The supposed French commitment to égalite masked a social snobbery that was as strong as the English with perhaps less commitment to opportunity.

Lavin had to seem respectful but in fact he thought that the man facing him was a martinet who knew little about policing any more, if he ever did, and was an expert in the bureaucratic politics in the upper reaches of French government. These areas were remote and inaccessible to citizens, organized groups, and many politicians. The inaccessibility helped explain why French interest groups, from taxi drivers to grain farmers and

civil servants would often resort to "direct action" in the
street against government.

M. Martain was not interested in Lavin's story. It
seemed to be full of conjectures about past events that
might or might not have occurred. Andrés Molnar may
have been a bad man, but his connection with jewel
thieves was uncertain. Besides, that was not a matter for
the Ministry of Foreign Affairs. The fact that his sons
were representatives of a Spanish bank was of no interest. The possibility that the Spanish bank could be using
illegal money in order to invest in the Picard bank was a
matter for the police and the Ministry of Finance. Finally,
the French police had no business reaching into Spanish
bank affairs.

"You might try Interpol," he said dismissively, and
turned his attention to papers on his desk, a signal for
Lavin to leave.

Lavin left with his proverbial tail between his legs as he
looked into another blind alley, but his most important vir-
tue as a policeman was that he never gave up. The Interpol
idea was a good one. He made an appointment to meet a
colleague at Interpol headquarters in Lyon and took the
train down in hopes of cooperation. The scenery on the
ride was pastoral France at its best, and he felt the nostalgia
of a country boy for the rural environment. He was now a
Parisian but had never fully become a city person. He was
an outsider in city or country. Maybe that was why he was
a good policeman. Outsiders are uncertain of all comers.

Chapter 5

The Interpol headquarters was a large gleaming glass building in Lyon, which was a bustling, prosperous city. Lavin knew only a few people there and went immediately by appointment to the office of Maurice Coors, a former colleague in Paris. Coors was a man of great experience, especially in European crime. He was heavyset from too much desk work, but quick on his feet and even quicker in his mind. Their conversation began with old memories of policing days in Paris, and they shared a laugh about their mutual contempt for Martain. Coors then listened to Lavin's tale carefully and told him what he knew. He had done some homework beforehand.

"Your suspicions of Molnar are well founded. He was involved with jewel thieves, but that was a long time ago. He escaped being prosecuted as a war criminal because he was protected as a member of Admiral Horthy's entourage, and Horthy was absolved of collaboration in war crimes. We do not know the source of Molnar's wealth in Portugal and Spain. He could have brought it with him from Hungary in 1945, and certainly Horthy had assets. It is also possible that the dictator of Portugal, Salazar, helped Horthy and his friends financially.

"It would be more difficult to link Molnar's assets to laundered or illegal money, particularly if the funds were invested in the Spanish bank. Those connections could be made if one could first find the criminal source of the money and then show factually how it was linked to Molnar and then invested.

"We will begin the inquiry with the justification that we are looking into illegal money laundering and also with the more tenuous suspicion of further inquiring into the purchase of shares in Picard's Paris bank, and even more tenuous suspicion of attempted murder. I will be able to persuade people here to do this solely on the strength of your strong reputation as an excellent policeman and a person of integrity. I will let you know if others agree, but a thorough investigation will take time. I would follow other leads in your case if I were you."

"Thank you old friend, you are good to help." Lavin felt a bond with Coors that he could not feel with Martain. They had come up through the ranks together.

Lavin thanked Coors and went back to Paris, asking himself which other leads to follow. He had followed the trails of the Spanish bank as far as he could go for the moment. The question of the bank in Tangier was open, but what should he do about it? He would follow developments with de Frontenac. There were two missing links with the past. One was Jean, Picard's natural, missing son, and his aunt and uncle. The other was Picard's personal history and the source of money that permitted him to invest in the bank.

He decided to follow Picard's trail. He was not president of the bank during the war. The handful of men who led the firm did not collaborate with the Germans or the Vichy regime. There was very little banking to do during the war except for deposits and some domestic business. The bank had survived into the postwar period because it had escaped any taint of collaboration and was in solid financial shape. Lavin thought that Picard's two brothers might help him learn more about their brother.

He took a train to Geneva to talk with Alain Picard after he had written ahead to make the arrangements. Picard could hardly refuse to see him since the detective was investigating his brother's death. Lavin found Alain and his wife, Catherine, living in a suburb of the city in a solid provincial cottage, surrounded by other retired French officers. The couple were well dressed and seemed very healthy for seventy-five-year-olds. Lavin recognized a type, almost for movie casting, of a French army officer. A small, neatly trimmed mustache perched on his upper lip and his black hair, with not a trace of gray, was sleeked down with pomade. Md. Picard was rather elegant in a flowered silk dress. Lavin thought that she was probably courteous with everyone as one might expect of a military wife.

Once they had settled at tea time with glasses of wine, Alain asked, "How can I help you? I have very little contact with my older brother in Montreal because he stayed in Paris during the war, and although he did not collaborate, he played no role in the Resistance as far as I know. My younger brother was never interested in anything except making money."

When Lavin asked if Picard knew where his brother found the money to invest in the bank, he received a scathing reply.

"There was no family money I can assure you because we didn't have any. Nor were there any rich relatives. It was a mystery to all of us."

The two brothers had seen each other infrequently in recent years. Alain's wife was a staunch Catholic who had been fond of Claude's wife but could not accept his taking a mistress. Neither of them knew anything of the whereabouts of her son and had never known his name or met him.

Lavin thanked them and left before he was subjected to the failures of France in surrendering its colonies, the materialism and lack of discipline in French society, and the decline of politics after de Gaulle. They were nice people with principles from the past. He was himself apolitical, accustomed to listening to all opinions without accepting any. If he had a creed, it was law and order. His opponents were criminals, and he was always unhappy until he solved a case.

His wife of thirty years, Sylvine, was a calming influence against his fierce energies. When he returned to their small but comfortable Paris apartment in the Marais, she asked him to list all his leads and assess their validity and ask what he might best do next.

"I must find out what happened to Jean Lucet and whether his aunt and uncle know, in fact, where he is. Could there be a connection between him and the death of his father?

"I must also talk with Pierre Picard in Montreal to learn what he might know about Jean Lucet.

"What is the Moroccan bank up to? Do the leaders have designs on taking control of the Paris bank from Lily de Frontenac? Surely it would not be necessary to kill her."

She listened sympathetically and advised him, "Let's take a weekend off and go see our daughter in the country."

They had just one daughter, Sophie, who lived in a small town on the coast of Normandy with her husband, a lawyer, and two children, whom their grandparents could never see enough. He agreed readily, and the next morning, Saturday, they directed their beloved Peugeot toward the coast. It was late November and the weather was still warm and clear.

Chapter 6

Veules-les-Roses was a hamlet on the Normandy coast south of Calais. Sophie Perrault and her husband, Anton, lived in a country house near the village. Anton practiced both civil and criminal law in nearby towns. Their two children, Adele and Jules, went to the local primary school. The charming village had a baker, a pastry shop, a bank, a police station, and a post office. It was supported by residents of the village and the nearby countryside.

The grandparents arrived in the afternoon and scooped up Adele and Jules in their arms with joy. Jules Lavin loved his daughter with a passion. She was pretty, smart, and a trained psychotherapist. Her open face and ready smile revealed a good listener. There were plenty of potential clients for her among the "worried well" in the larger community. She had an office at the side of her home, and her husband and children had learned not to look at clients as they went to and from their cars to her door. Anton had a wide practice, mostly of small businessmen who required legal help, plus the usual wills and domestic disputes, but he also defended the few people who were charged with crime, often petty offenses.

Lavin had discussed his cases with them in the past, but his wife had directed him not to bring his problems to them on this trip, so the first night was spent around the table and a good meal with news about their lives, particularly the grandchildren. There was great warmth in the family circle. They ate in the kitchen at a round table, and a large stone fireplace provided burning, crackling logs. The two poodles, one black and the other brown, brother and sister, seemed to listen to the conversation. Affectionate dogs enhance the closeness of a company.

The seniors slept well and came down to a breakfast of croissants, jam and butter, and country ham, with rich, hot coffee. The detective had forgotten his worries temporarily. After breakfast Lavin took a walk through the village with his son-in-law. The women had given them shopping directions, which they dutifully carried out. When they had finished, they stood on the breakwater and looked at the ocean, both seemingly lost in thought. Anton broke the silence,

"What are you working on these days?"

It was an innocent question, and Lavin was unable to put it off or delay an answer. He hoped for advice.

"I am investigating a murder and attempted murder

of a father and the attempted murder of his daughter. My problem is that I have too many leads, none of which seem to go anywhere. I need an event or a break of some kind."

Anton was able to pull all the details of the case out of his father-in-law, and as a modest practitioner of criminal law, he was interested.

"You are waiting on information about your Hungarian and the two banks. The matter of jewel thieves is murky. Why don't you follow the threads about Claude Picard more fully? I would like to know what happened to his illegitimate son. People do not just disappear. They can usually be found with enough effort. This boy, who is now grown up, may not have friendly feelings about the father who rejected him but,

"It is hard for me to believe that the aunt and uncle know nothing of his whereabouts," Lavin replied. "If they were close, they would still be close. But there may be a good reason why he wishes to stay hidden, and they will respect that. Let's go back and ask Sophie. She knows about families."

After they returned to the house Anton brought up the issue immediately to Sophie, and it all came out before Sylvine could prevent it. Lavin was in a very relaxed mood so she decided that he might actually learn from the advice he received. He told the whole story again and waited for his daughter to respond. She asked a number of questions about the Picard family, his children and brothers, and then made some suggestions.

"From your description of Jean Lucet's aunt and uncle, I cannot think that he would leave them without staying in touch. These were the only family he had, and he needed them emotionally as a young person of seventeen. It is not an easy thing to voluntarily make yourself an orphan and divorce oneself from a family that you care for and cares for you. I would go back to his aunt and uncle and press them to be forthcoming. If he is hiding and they know that and see a justified reason for it, then you will have at least learned something.

"If you want to talk to him because he may have had something to do with his father's death, they may suspect something as well or know something, in which case they will be uncooperative. You should be able to sense that."

Lavin listened carefully. He could foresee a difficult conversation with the aunt and uncle, particularly because they would surely think that he suspected their nephew of something. On the other hand, if they cooperated, they could clear Jean Lucet of any suspicion. He would appeal to them accordingly, if need be.

There was no more discussion of the matter for the rest of the weekend. Lavin relaxed as much as he could and enjoyed himself. He recognized that if he tightened up again and felt the pressure that he had been imposing on himself, he would be a poorer detective. His work was best when it proceeded with relaxed confidence rather than with compulsive force. He would have to charm Marie and Gilles Beauvais by slow persuasion rather than by forced demands. They would have no reason to cooperate unless they could see it was in Jean's best interests. He had to face the fact that they might not agree, but then he would have suspicions to follow up. "Le weekend," as the French telecasters say it, had relaxed him greatly. It was happiest when he was with his family. Sylvine thought that the advice made sense and urged him on the drive back to Paris, to appeal to the sympathy of the aunt and uncle for their nephew rather than take a hard line.

He woke up in Paris on Monday morning with a quiet resolve to find Lucet. There could be a motive of revenge against Picard for disowning him and even against Lily for inheriting part of what he thought to be rightfully his. He would have to proceed very carefully and not appear to be suspecting a person he did not know as a criminal. At this point Jean Lucet was only a person of interest.

He called Marie and Gilles Beauvais and asked if he might meet once more. Each questioned why it was necessary and also asked why he wanted to see them together. He thought about trying to trap them separately but decided to appeal to their feelings and reason as an aunt and uncle. He would open with civility and then press harder if he thought that they were holding back what they knew about their nephew. They both seemed nervous to him, and this enabled him to appear calm as if to appear to be in control. He began in the way that he had rehearsed with his wife.

"I would really like to talk with your nephew. I do not

suspect him of a crime, but he may very well know something about his father, Claude Picard, that would help us find his killer. We need to know everything that we can find out about Picard's history, and Jean may have learned something from his mother, or from some other person, that would help me in this case.

"You have told me that you have lost track of Jean, but I find difficult to believe that he would not want to keep in touch with you. You are his only family. By the same token he is your only family. Neither of you is married or has children, and I cannot really believe that you would let him go without urging him to stay in touch or trying to find him were he to disappear.

"You may think that you are protecting him from something or someone, perhaps his father's killers, especially since Lily was attacked. If so, the best way to help him is to find the killers. I promise that if you tell me where he is, I will not violate his privacy or confidentiality."

A long pause ensued, and they looked at each other carefully. Finally Marie waved her hand toward Gilles, as if to say, go on. So Gilles began, with some hesitancy.

"Jean wanted to attend a university, but he needed his father's help, and that was not to be had. So he searched for another source of help and found one. It was Claude Picard's older brother, Pierre, the lawyer in Montreal. Marie and I knew that there were two brothers, but we did not know either of them, even by name. We also did not know that he knew them. Evidently he did, and

Pierre had taken an interest in him over the years. Jean wrote Pierre, and the reply was 'come to Canada and I will help you.'"

"So before we knew it, Jean was off to Montreal. He wrote us from time to time as he attended the Université de Montréal and its school of commerce. He lived with his uncle. His father knew nothing about this, as far as we know. When he graduated, he went to work for a bank in Montreal, which he seemed to enjoy, but we have not heard from him for some time. To the best of our knowledge, he is still there.

"We did not want you to know this because we wished to protect him from you in case he was involved in a crime, to be honest. We also wanted to protect him in case anyone wished to harm him, for his father had been murdered and his sister almost killed. We are guilty of withholding evidence but not of a crime, as such, and we hope that you will understand."

Lavin answered that he understood, but he did not excuse them. The important thing was that he could now find and talk with Jean. He would write or perhaps call him. It might be necessary to bring Jean back to France or to go see him in Montreal. After this discussion, they sat and talked for some time about Jean.

"He is a very intense young man," said Marie, "who resented his father's indifference deeply. He would try to talk with his father and get acquainted. Claude was perfectly polite and would talk with him, but he never offered to do anything for him. Anne was always in hopes that he would help Jean, but she dared not make strong claims for Jean because she was dependent on Claude for support. She was his mistress, and he expected special favors and, in their later years, companionship and affection. He was not a bad man, and Anne loved him in a way. We learned from her that he had not had an easy early life. Neither his father nor his mother was good to the three sons. The parents were concerned primarily with themselves, their own security, and their status as minor aristocracy. She had told them that Claude felt himself to be virtually orphaned at an early age. The fact that he survived and made a smooth transition into the Parisian business world before the war, and then prospered in it afterward, showed his resilience and increased his self-confidence. But he always saw himself to be alone. He had to protect himself in a cruel world."

Gilles added,

"This explained why he did not help his son. Each man was to make his own way. Claude would not help others who could help themselves. He expected Jean to fight his way up as he had, with ambition and talent. It would spoil him to help him."

Neither of them liked Picard. They had gotten to know him through Anne, but he had never shown much interest in them. He was very dependent on Anne for his emotional life. She softened the insecurity that fired his aggressiveness. He was desolate when she died, but once she was gone, there was nothing left for him. He regarded Jean not as a consolation but a burden.

Lavin was grateful for their honesty, thanked them, and promised to let them know how their nephew, Jean Lucet, was doing, if he found out. He told them that he would call Montreal right away. He returned to his office and did just that.

Chapter 7

It was noon in Paris and seven at night in Montreal. Lavin found Pierre Picard through information and dialed the number. A woman answered in French, and he asked for Jean Lucet. She paused and then said, "I will call my husband." A man came to the phone and said that he was Pierre Picard. Lavin had not met him because Pierre had not come to France for his brother's funeral, having made his excuses to Lily. Lavin had not paid much attention to that fact at the time.

"Jean is not here at present. May I ask who is calling?"

"I am Inspector Jules Lavin of the French Sûreté in Paris, and I am in charge of the investigation of the murder of your brother Claude. My inquiries carry me far afield, even to Canada. I have learned that Jean Lucet is in Montreal from his aunt and uncle and wish to talk with him about the death of his father. Do you expect him back soon?"

Picard did not hesitate. It occurred to Lavin that he might not know that his nephew was missing in France.

"Inspector, I am happy to help you in your work, but Jean recently left Montreal on temporary assignment from his bank here to a French bank in Buenos Aires. The bank is seeking more South American business, and there is a large French-speaking community in Argentina. I can give you his address if you wish."

Lavin asked Picard to describe the circumstances in which his nephew had come to Canada.

"I would visit Paris over the years on business, as an attorney, and would see my brother Claude. We were not close, but I could not go there without seeing him. I liked his wife and his two children. They were my niece and nephew and nice young people. I also became acquainted with Anne Beauvais after Claude's wife died. He was not keen to introduce me, but I insisted. I knew that she had a son, who was also my nephew, and I wanted to know him. His mother, Anne, was a charming woman, an actress and specialist in comedy, who could charm a bird out of a tree. The boy, Jean, who took his mother's last name, was appealing as a youngster. He was quiet and well mannered and very serious. I was told that he was an excellent student. As he grew up, we became well acquainted, and I developed great affection for him.

"Then his mother died. She had not been well, but she

died quickly. Claude, who was not an emotional person, was devastated. One would think that her death would bind him closer to his son, but that did not happen. He had never tried to get close to the boy, and it seemed too late for him to try. He could not turn on a centime emotionally.

"Claude was not willing to support Jean for his university education. This devastated his son. He wanted a father. We corresponded about all this, and finally I offered to help him if he would come to Montreal. He accepted, and we took him in. He lived with us and went to the Université de Montréal, doing very well and getting himself a good position of the Bank of Montreal as an investment officer.

"He is not here now because six months ago the bank sent him to a bank in Buenos Aires on temporary assignment. The Bank of Montreal has developed investment relations with the big bank there with French-speaking clients. We hear from him from time to time. He is enjoying the work but intends to return home before too long. He is very much a French speaker, and I cannot imagine him living in that kind of environment for very long."

Picard gave Lavin the addresses and telephone numbers that he needed, and afterward he asked the detective what more he knew about his brother's death.

Lavin replied,

"It remains a mystery. We have not discovered enemies or possible motives from those who knew him. Other financial institutions wish to invest in the bank, but such motives are not likely to lead to murder. I do not suspect your nephew but hope that he may know something about aspects of Picard's life that we do not know. That is a long shot, but I am grasping at straws for the moment."

Picard promised to forward anything that he might learn from his business interests in France, and they said a pleasant good-bye.

The next day Lavin called the bank in Buenos Aires and asked for Jean Lucet. The voice that answered reported that Mr. Lucet had completed his work with the bank and returned to Montreal. Lavin pressed the question to a top officer of the bank, who confirmed the report.

"He did very good work for us and helped develop our future relations with the Bank of Montreal in a very solid way. We look forward to future collaboration with him."

The difficulty for Lavin was that Jean Lucet had left Buenos Aires one month before, but he was not in Montreal. He checked with Pierre Picard again; he had heard nothing. Picard and his wife were sure that if the young man had taken a vacation, they have known about it. A further check with Jean's superiors at the Bank of Montreal revealed that he had been granted an extended leave to study banking at the London Business School, located in Regents Park, London. A call to the London Business School produced the reply that he was not expected until the new term began in September. They had only the Montreal address for him. Lavin was grinding his teeth again.

Grasping at straws again he decided that he might learn something, anything, if he looked at the bank in Tangier and its interest in investing in the Picard bank. Could it be possible that Jean Lucet was involved in some way in investments in Picard's bank? Perhaps he was trying to establish his identity through an indirect route? This was a wild thought, but Lavin liked to follow his intuition, often with surprising results. He went to see de Frontenac and asked him who was representing the bank in Tangier.

"There are two men with whom I meet. They have come to Paris recently" de Frontenac answered. "The senior man is of English background although he has never been in England. His mother was English also, but she had not lived in England. Her parents had lived in Tangier for a long time. There is a Moroccan who is trilingual, Arabic, French, and English. He is a lawyer who understands legal aspects of any merger."

De Frontenac told Lavin that he and his wife, Lily, were receptive to the offers of the Tangier bank because they wished to invest without asking for partnership. Lily's brother Marc was pushing them to go through with the investment because the foundation funded by the bank was supporting his research. He did not see a quid pro quo but simply wanted to help the bank, which had been good to him, through the foundation.

Lavin had no official reason to approach the bank. It was not involved in any crime. He did not tell either de Frontenac or Lily of his intuition because he might uncover evidence of a crime, and he did not want to raise the matter of Jean Lucet with them. It was all speculation on his part. He thought of asking Marc to look into things but pulled back. The best thing to do was to call the president of the bank in Tangier and ask him directly about Jean Lucet. He placed a call and was told that M. Edouard Lesage was traveling but would call him on his return in two days. Inquiry revealed that Lesage was of French birth but was long a resident in Tangier. He returned the call two days later.

"What can I do for you, Inspector?"

"This is a delicate matter, M. Lesage. I am investigating the murder of M. Claude Picard, a case with which you are familiar. He had an illegitimate son who was educated in Canada, became a banker with the Bank of Montreal, and then worked recently with the Bank of France in Buenos Aires. He has disappeared. I am speculating that he may surfaced somewhere recently in connection with his father's bank in Paris. Do you have anyone in your bank who meets such a description?"

Lesage replied that Jean Lucet had recently joined his staff. He was an expert in mergers and acquisitions and, for that reason, had been assigned to future discussions with the Picard bank in Paris. He had come with high recommendations from the Bank of Montreal. This information puzzled Lavin because that bank told him that Lucet was on leave in London. Further questions and an inquiry revealed that the letter from the Bank of Montreal had come from the chief counsel of the bank, Pierre Picard. What the letter had said was perhaps true, but it had been written under false pretenses by Picard, as if he were speaking for the Bank of Montreal.

Lavin decided that he must see Lucet in person. He had not committed a crime as such. He was an expert in mergers and acquisitions. But he was up to something. The team of the Moroccan bank was not due to come to Paris for another two months so Lavin decided that he had to go to Tangier. He would call on Lucet at the bank and confront him with the facts. Doing this seemed better than calling at his home, a less structured situation.

Tangier is an old city going back to the Phoenicians, Greeks, and Romans. It sits on the North African Atlantic coast directly across from the Rock of Gibraltar. It was a free city from 1923 until taken over by the new nation of Morocco in 1956. Its European population was large, perhaps twenty percent European, along with Arabs, Berbers, and other North African groups. It had been under French oversight by treaty agreement between France and Spain after 1912 until 1956. French was the language used in large businesses, including banks. The bank where Lucet was working was only one of such institutions.

The city itself was small and compact, surrounded by

sprawling suburbs. Its architecture was colonial French and Spanish adapted to Arab style. The streets were small and crowded, and taxis had to fight their way. Lavin flew in at mid-day and took a cab to his hotel. His thoughts matched the jumble of architecture and the narrow and tangled streets and traffic he saw out of the cab window. He was a clear thinker and the boulevards and round-abouts of Paris matched his mind. Once in his hotel, he called Lesage to say that he was going to the bank to meet Lucet and asked Lesage to have men on hand should any difficulties arise. He did not anticipate any problems.

The bank building was a quasi-monumental copy of the kind found in Paris in the business districts. It surely dated from before the First World War. The lobby was an open space surrounded by grilled windows for trans-actions with customers, several of them with signs indi-cating the language to be used. A kiosk in the center purported to be the key to directions. Lavin approached a young Arab woman and asked, in French, for directions to the office of M. Jean Lucet. She gave him the floor and the office number and asked if he wished to be an-nounced. He replied that there was no need. He found the door to the office on the fifth floor and entered. It was a suite with secretaries for several bank officers. A placard in front of a young woman had Lucet's name on it. Lavin asked if he might see M. Lucet and told her that he was an Inspector of the Sûreté Nationale from Paris when she asked him. She made no expression but rose and walked down a back corridor. She might have used the telephone, but she did not. After a few minutes she returned and told him that M. Lucet would see him and gave directions. He walked down the corridor and faced an open door.

"Come in, Inspector," said a young man with sandy hair, blue eyes, and a brown complexion. "If you saw pictures of my mother, you would know me. I do not look like my father in the least."

Lavin was taken aback that Jean's demeanor was so open and frank. He could only say, "I have been trying to find you."

"And you have succeeded at last. I have not been running from you, although my uncle Pierre told me of your visit to Montreal. I have been on a pursuit of my own, which has nothing to do with you or my father's murder. But how did you find me?"

He asked the inspector to sit down, and Lavin told him of the crooked path that he had followed.

"Congratulations. You are a very clever policeman. I will be glad to explain what I am doing here and why, but please tell me what you have wanted to know from me."

"I have so few leads to who might have killed your father that I thought that you might know something about his past that would have helped me go on."

Lucet replied,

"I did not know him well. He would come to the country to see my mother and often stay for a week or two at a time. And then she would go off to Paris to see him. They took trips together, usually in Europe, but sometimes to England and America.

"He was always pleasant with me, but distant as if I were a nephew that he did not know well. He would ask me about my school work but never about my plans for a career or my future life.

"I was devastated when my mother died because suddenly I was all alone. I had known that she was ill, but neither he nor my aunt and uncle knew how sick she was or that she would die so suddenly. My aunt and uncle are wonderful people, and I lived with Aunt Marie immediately after my mother's death. My father made arrangements to sell her house immediately and asked me to leave. He said that he would not be able to help me financially because of his other obligations, especially the education of his two children. He was cold-blooded about it. I did not see what I could do. I wanted to go to university, but one needs financial help. I wrote my uncle Pierre in Montreal, and he offered to help me. We had met a number of times over the years when he had come to France. He liked my mother a great deal and would always call on her and of course see me. He showed an interest in me that my father had never shown."

Lavin was much surprised to find Lucet so forthcoming. He responded by saying, "I have been trying to find you as a kind of a puzzle, almost for its own sake. Why have you engaged in this elaborate subterfuge to take leave from the Bank of Montreal, ostensibly to attend Oxford and then return to Montreal, and yet you are here working for the Bank of France in Tangier?"

Lucet smiled and resumed:

"I had no such intention when I went to Argentina. But then my uncle told me of my father's death and that my half sister, whom I had never met, would direct the bank. I began to wonder if I might join the family, as a blood relation, and perhaps play a part in the bank itself. My strongest desire was to be accepted by my sister and brother. They are my family, and I have felt the loneliness of separation all my life."

"Why did you not just approach them directly?" asked Lavin.

"I thought about it, but I did not know them and was afraid that they would see me as an opportunist trying to trade on my past. For all I knew, they were like my father. I decided that I needed some leverage. I followed news of international banking closely, and when I read that the Bank of France in Tangier was seeking investment in the family bank in Paris I decided to apply for a position here, and I got the job. My uncle's letter helped me a great deal. I never intended to go to Oxford and will perhaps resign from the Bank of Montreal even if nothing happens with the overture to Paris. I will think again about how to approach the family if that fails. I have met my half brother here in Tangier by showing an interest in his research, which is supported by the bank's foundation. I might begin with him."

This story had so astonished Lavin that he was at a loss for words:

"I am beyond my limitations as a policeman and cannot advise you what to do. I have met your sister and her husband. They appear to be decent people. She told me the story of your father and mother and expressed an interest in knowing your whereabouts. Your aunt and uncle, who care for you deeply, think that you are still in Montreal, and you surely wish to stay in touch with them.

"There is evidently support in Paris and here for a new relationship between the two banks. I have an idea. You would tell your story to M. Lesage, the president of your bank, and volunteer to complete the transaction as a part of which you tell your family who you are."

Lucet looked intently at Lavin for a long moment and then smiled, saying,

"You are an expert about crime, Inspector, and you are also an expert reader of people. I think that you are absolutely right. My uncle in Montreal would surely agree with your advice."

They agreed that they would ask to see Edouard Lesage, the bank president, immediately. Lucet called Lesage's secretary and explained that he and Inspector Lavin wished to see the president right away on a most important matter. Lesage had been alerted by Lavin and sent word that they were to come upstairs immediately. In a few minutes they entered his large office on the top floor of the bank whose windows spanned the wide view of the city in every direction. It was a penthouse office. Lesage had left his large desk bordered by Moroccan artifacts and was seated in one of three white chairs drawn up with a view of the ocean. He rose to greet them, almost as if he expected good news. They shook hands, and all sat down at his invitation.

He began, "I assume that you have a story to tell me," and he settled back to listen.

Jean began to slowly tell his story, working backward from his time in Argentina, and then explaining how he had gotten to Montreal and his experience there. He finished with an account of his life in France and his relationship with the Picard family. Lavin interpreted at times, helping to explain how he had followed the trail to find Jean. Lesage sat quietly with deep interest, saying nothing until they finished.

"I suppose the question before us is what we do now. You must decide what to do about your brother and sister. My charge is to pursue the best interests of the bank. I gather that you think," addressing Lavin, "that those interests are compatible, that a recognition and gathering of siblings will enhance the partnership between the banks."

Lavin nodded that he agreed, but Lesage went on, "What if the Picards, brother and sister and son-in-law, see Jean as an interloper who has deceived us all in pursuit of his selfish interests?"

Lavin answered that he thought that this would not happen. "I know Lily, not well, but she expressed a desire to know about her missing brother. Neither she nor her husband seems at all like her father, as he has been described to me. You know her brother Marc and his advocacy of the union between the banks. Surely he would help move things along."

At that point Jean spoke up again: "I have met Marc several times and find him very likable. What if I reveal myself to him before we make any overture to Paris? If he accepts me, he will probably be open to our plans."

Lesage concurred in this idea: "Marc is working on his project about fifty miles from here. It is pretty desolate country, but one can easily drive to the site. I can call and tell him of Jean's future importance in the negotiations and say that Jean would like to talk with him. It might be a good idea if Inspector Lavin accompanied you to confirm your story. We will tell Marc that the Inspector is on a different errand about his investigation and that they happen to be coming together."

All agreed, and the meeting broke up with the understanding that the adventure would begin the next day.

The next morning Jean and Lavin climbed into a jeep with a top for shade on top and an Arab driver. He knew where he was going as they passed through small towns and villages. The road was paved, after a fashion, with potholes here and there. The land was desolate, not desert but flat, dry earth. It was uninteresting country but both men were keyed up because the immediate future was unknown but perhaps exciting. They eventually arrived at the camp and saw a few tents bolstered by wood frames at their bases and what appeared to be big holes in the ground. These were the so-called digs. The project was the excavation of an old palace. It could have been Berber, Carthaginian, Christian, or Moorish and perhaps historic layers of many traditions and periods. They parked the jeep near a small frame building that might be an office and walked in.

"We are looking for Marc Picard," Jean said to a young woman with long scraggly hair and a baseball cap on her head. On closer inspection it was a Yankees cap. Jean had seen Yankee caps wherever he traveled. She was shuffling papers as they walked in but looked up and said in what might have been a German accent in French:

"He is out on the dig now. Would you like me to go get him, or do you want to walk toward him?"

They answered that they would find him if she would point the way, which she did.

"He will have a red bandana around his forehead," she added. "Just call out to him."

They did not walk very far before they came to a good-sized excavation in which people were digging and brushing surfaces and objects that seemed to have come from the ground. A man with sandy hair and a red bandana was standing in the center, seemingly in touch with each of them. He was examining an object with two young women at the moment. Lavin concluded that most of the people were graduate students and research assistants. Marc was the major domo.

They had not discussed how to approach a conversation with him and were feeling their way so they just called out his name. He looked up, waved, and answered, asking if they could speak with him at the top. He quickly climbed a dirt staircase up to their level. When he got to the top, he recognized Lavin, whom he had met in Paris after his father's funeral. He also acknowledged Lucet by name but did not ask why he was there.

"I assume that you are here on business," Marc said, "but this is far afield, isn't it?"

"It would seem so," Lavin replied, "but there have been new developments. Is there a comfortable, private place where we can talk?"

"We live in tents, but there is an air-conditioned trailer where we keep documents and cash and so on," Marc replied.

He led the way to a large trailer, and they settled into a cool interior in deck chairs. Now it was time for one of them to say something, and they hesitated.

Lavin finally began with a sort of question, "You are aware that you and your sister have a half brother that you have never met?"

Marc looked quickly at Jean but said nothing.

"I have been searching for him for some time, in France, Montreal, and Argentina, and I have finally found him here in Tangier."

He did not say that Jean was the man, but Marc asked Jean,

"Are you my brother?"

"I am," replied Jean with a smile.

Marc rose and shook Jean's hand and almost embraced him.

"How does this come to be?"

Jean told him the story of his mother and father, of his life in Canada with their uncle, and how he had come to Tangier.

"I could have approached you directly," he said, "but I was not sure how you would respond so I have come this roundabout way."

"You could have come to me in any way that you wished, and I would have welcomed you with open arms. I am sure that my sister will feel the same way. We knew your mother slightly. She was a lovely person. We never felt right about the way our father treated you. We knew nothing about you or about his relationship with you, but it bothered us. We tried to raise the issue, but he would never discuss it. Your appearance closes the circle on a painful experience for all of us."

With this Marc embraced his brother, and Lavin knew that his work was done. Marc called Lily, told her the good news, which she welcomed, and he and Jean left for Tangier and the flight for Paris. When they arrived at the De Gaulle Airport, Lavin excused himself and went home. He still had a murder and an attempted murder to solve. He assumed, without knowing, that the Beauvais brother and sister would be happily included in the celebrations.

He also assumed that there would be a future place in the Paris bank for Jean. He learned later that this was the case and that the agreement with the bank in Tangier had been completed. Pierre Picard called to thank him and see him the next time that he was in Paris. This was all to the good, but meanwhile . . .

Chapter 8

Lavin had done his good deed, but that would not satisfy his superiors. He had to catch a murderer. It was late November. The case was three months old, and it was getting cold. He got in touch with Maurice Coors at Interpol to see if they had learned anything else about Andrés Molnar. Coors came on the phone.

"We have done some more digging into Molnar's history. The jewel thieves whom he fronted for in Paris in 1927 had their headquarters in Marseille, and the organization survived the war. There was a lot of business for them on the Riviera, even during the war, and certainly afterward. After the war they began to launder their profits in ordinary businesses, and this is where Molnar comes in. He went to Portugal with money, and we do not know the source. But he seems to have invested in companies in which laundered money was also invested, e.g., a shipping firm owned by émigré Hungarians.

"His two sons now own and manage an investment firm that puts its money into a variety of enterprises. They are Spanish nationals who work in Paris and Marseille. They use their mother's maiden name, Ramirez. We have just begun to investigate them, and I would rather that you do not approach them until we know more."

Lavin could hardly believe his ears. The Ramirez brothers were the agents for the Spanish bank that wished to invest in Picard's firm. This seemed to be a stroke of luck. What was he to do with it? He was not happy to wait, but in the meantime he called on Paul de Frontenac to ask about other possible investors in the bank. De Frontenac told him of an inquiry from an investment firm in Marseille. This was too much for Lavin. The Molnar brothers were behind both offers. Their identities were not hidden, but what were they up to? He called Coors and told him of the situation.

"I must talk to these brothers. Can we think of a way in which I can approach them about Picard's death without imposing on your investigation?"

Coors said that he might approach the brothers as part of a very wide-ranging investigation into Picard's murder, but he must be very circumspect. Lavin agreed. Yet how he would justify his approach, especially as a detective? He decided to tell them that he was trying to understand Picard's life and history and that Picard had known their father in Paris in the nineteen twenties.. Did they know anything about Picard's history that might help explain why someone would kill him in the 1980s? He knew it was a weak excuse, but he wanted to meet and talk with the brothers in hopes of finding something hidden in their motives or their offers.

Carlos and Juan Ramirez agreed to meet him in Marseille in two weeks. He took the high-speed train from Paris on a weekday morning and got off at the station near the grand Fountain Castellane. He took a taxi through the crowded streets to the Police Prefecture in the 6th Arrondissement. It was the standard custom to inform his colleagues of his mission. He had already informed them with a message, but he wanted to see possible colleagues should he need their help in the future. He had worked with some of the people there but was asked to meet a man he did not know, Francois Benoit. After they met, Lavin asked him,

"Is there any particular reason why you are meeting me?"

"There may be. We suspect that the Molnar brothers may have ties with a Corsican crime syndicate. They go to Corsica occasionally, ostensibly on business, but they do very little business with Corsican firms. We do not think that they are taking vacations. They go there singly. But no one comes to Marseille from Corsica to see them.

"We can find no sign that the brothers are active as criminals. Rather we suspect that they could be investing criminal money in various enterprises. But we have no proof. The chains of connection to original investors are long and circuitous. So far we have not been able to run any of this to ground."

Lavin realized that he was probably going to be dealing with very skillful and perhaps slippery people as he took a cab to the Molnar brothers' office in a nondescript building. The office was near the Centre Bourse, the main shopping mall of the city. He entered the building and took an elevator to the fifth floor. The people in the hallways and elevator appeared to be typical French business people. The sign on the wooden door of their office read "Ramirez Enterprises." He entered to find no one there, not even a secretary or a desk for a secretary. A middle-aged man emerged from a door and said, "M. Lavin?" When Lavin acknowledged himself, the man said,

"I am Carlos Ramirez. Please come in."

He then turned and led Lavin into a corridor that opened into a suite with a wide window and a view of the city's harbor. Another man sitting in the room rose and introduced himself as Juan Ramirez. He seemed a little older than his brother. Both men looked slightly Spanish, but they could have been from anywhere in southern Europe. They did not look Hungarian to Lavin, although he was not sure what Hungarians looked like. He had never been to eastern Europe.

Juan spoke first: "We wish to assist you in any way that we might, but it is not clear to us how we might help."

Lavin replied, "I am looking into as much as I can about Picard's life. This includes his business affairs and his personal life. I know that your father was a friend of his in Paris in 1926, and here you are dealing with him and his bank in 1988. It is a small world."

"We know nothing about that friendship," said Carlos. "That was long before we were born."

Lavin had first learned of the friendship from the American John Page, who had learned of it from Katie. The Interpol information confirmed Molnar's association with jewel thieves in 1927, but Lavin could not assert this directly.

"Your father went to Portugal in 1945 with money in that he supported himself and eventually your mother and the two of you. Do you know the basis of his income after he went to Portugal?"

"No," Juan replied, "and what business is that of yours? That can have no connection with your case." Juan said this stridently, rising from his chair as if to stand up.

Lavin saw that he had overreached. "I apologize. It is just that Picard received a large sum of money from an unknown source in the 1920s, which enabled him to purchase a share in his bank."

"Well, we know nothing about that," added Carlos.

Lavin shifted his focus: "How does it happen that you are trying to buy shares in the Paris bank in which you represent two different entities, the bank in Madrid and investors in your own firm?"

"We act as agents for investors whoever they may be," Juan said. "The Spanish bank approached us first. It is our business to act as financial agents. The other group of investors came in later. We had to get the permission of the bank in Spain to act for both parties. They saw it as in their interest because they wish to dilute the share of the Picard family in the bank. The second investment is much smaller than the Spanish one. They know in Madrid who our investors are and have not raised any objections."

The brothers were clearly uncomfortable with his questions and began to shift their legs and look at their watches. Lavin was not getting anywhere. He began to gamble.

"Where did you get the capital to start your investment firm? Was it from your father?"

"This is not any of your business," they both exclaimed simultaneously, and then Juan added, "I think that this meeting is over." They both rose.

Lavin would not give up:

"Tell me about your business in Corsica."

They both sat down. "What do you know?" Carlos asked.

"The police think that you may be laundering money that is perhaps not of the highest quality in your work as agents," he replied.

Juan said emphatically, "We invest funds that come to us from a variety of sources, and we do not always know the initial source of the money. But we do know about the honesty and reliability of the final investors who come to us. We act as agents, and we take only commissions rather than profits from investments." He added,

"There is one Corsican client about whom we have some doubts because his money is Algerian and the character of the investors is not at all clear."

Lavin asked him to say more.

"We know little about the firm in Corsica. They came to us without any introduction. We have placed their money in the proposed investment in the Paris bank. We would like to know more before we work with them again."

Lavin replied, "There may be no problem, but the Marseille police are interested in money laundering, and I am bound to let them know whatever I learn. I do not suspect you of any involvement in Picard's murder. Your attempt to invest in his bank seems straightforward. We will check your story with the bank in Madrid. I would appreciate any information you could give me about your client in Corsica."

The brothers were reluctant, but relieved to be free from his inquiries, they named the Corsican firm and its address. Lavin left, disappointed that he was no closer to finding Picard's killer.

He reported to his colleagues in Marseille, knowing that they would follow the story of the brothers to wherever it led, and he took the train back to Paris. His mood was bleak. What more could he do that he had not done?

Chapter 9

Once back in Paris, Lavin called the Spanish bank and asked them to verify their scrutiny of the investment record of the Ramirez brothers. He received a pro forma reply, but when there was no response after a week, he called the president of the bank, Alfred Cruz. Cruz had not been told of the request but promised to comply as soon as the necessary information could be discovered. He called back two weeks later:

"M. Lavin, there is something that we do not like about the Corsican investor. We cannot trace the origin of the money. The Ramirez brothers are right to raise questions. They listed this investor to us as legitimate and did not tell us of the doubts they expressed to you. You put the kind of pressure on them, as a policeman, that we could have done but did not do. Had we had such doubts we might have canceled our contract with them. As it is, I think that I will do so in a backhanded way. Negotiations with the Paris bank are stalled. We will tell them in Paris that we will reconsider our offer and perhaps revise it. We will let the Ramirez brothers go and not go back to them should we reopen negotiations. Please keep all this confidential, and thank you for your help."

Lavin kept solving other people's problems but was getting nowhere with his own. He called François Benoît in Marseille and asked to be informed if anything developed about the Corsicans. There could still be a connection to the Paris murder although he had only his imagination to go on. Every base had to be covered again and again. He also called John Page to ask if he had received any more letters. Page had no news. He and his wife had kept in touch with Katie and Lavin decided that he must do the same, so he called on her. She was as gracious as

"Can you remember anything about Claude Picard in his life, as you knew him, that might give me a clue as to any antagonisms or enemies that he might have had?"

Katie replied that she had not known him well, only socially. She knew his first wife somewhat better and liked her, but had not known his mistress. He might have had difficulty making his way in financial affairs, however, had it not been for the unexpected and unexplained money from a secret source. He claimed that the gift was from a relative, and no one denied it so the matter was forgotten.

"I do remember that he was very strong in his defense

of French Algeria and very much in opposition to De Gaulle's actions in 1959 to free Algeria and France from the colonial burden. He was a fervent advocate for French Indochina and publicly opposed the Geneva Treaty in 1954 in which France withdrew from Southeast Asia. I assumed that this was just his right-wing politics, of which there was a great deal in France in the 1950s. I think that his father was quite active in right wing politics before the war and that Claude was of the same persuasion."

This information interested Lavin. He would look for any possible political aspect of the murder, even though it took place more than thirty years after those events. What might have triggered memories of events of the past?

As long as he was looking into the past, he decided to continue in that vein and called Paul de Frontenac for an appointment. Lily and her husband were virtually co-executives. He did not want to bother her with inquiries about her father's banking history so he called her husband. De Frontenac's office was rich in furnishings—a thick dark blue rug with handsome Oriental throw rugs in places. The wood paneling was mellow burnished brown, and the window drapes were dark red, set off by light yellow curtains. All the chairs were brown leather, some stationary and some on wheels. De Frontenac had an aristocratic name, but Lavin knew that his father had purchased the name from a family without heirs in the 1950s. This practice was not uncommon. The former president of France, Valery Giscard d'Estaing, inherited the same benefit.

"I was wondering," asked Lavin, "if one might find evidence in Claude Picard's management of the bank over the years that might give some suggestions about people who might have wanted to do him harm, perhaps not kill him, but harm him in some way."

De Frontenac listened carefully, paused, and then said, "I will ask Lily about such possibilities from her personal knowledge, but I will also look back at past cases where Picard might have said no to people, offended or angered them, or let them down in any way. But this makes me nervous, Inspector. An aggrieved party is not a murderer. You would have to be very careful about approaching any such people."

"I understand that. I cannot question people about a murder out of the blue. There would have to be a strong suspicion of a motive for murder."

He went back to the Sûreté with the assurance that de Frontenac would call him if anything should turn up. In his office he stewed and stewed in his own ignorance and frustration. He had done excellent police work, despite major obstacles. Unless he had a break he would fail, and he had never failed to solve a case. He could understand how some policemen "fixed" facts so that someone would be blamed for a crime and they would get the credit. One could not fail to solve a crime, and success only came with a solution.

De Frontenac called in a few days. He said, "There are two recent instances in which my father-in-law angered clients. Lily and I were involved in both of them. The first was a case in which a prominent textile manufacturer, an old family firm with long financial support from the bank, was denied a large loan for reinvestment in the modernization of manufacturing machinery. M. Picard had known the family well for a generation, but he had personally vetoed the loan and so informed the family.

"The other instance was his refusal to contribute bank funds for the support of an established private foundation for pensions for retired French military officers. The director of the foundation, who had long known my father-in-law, was furious, wrote him a scathing letter, and complained bitterly to Lily. But there was nothing she could do."

Lavin thanked him and began to look at the textile firm in question. It bore the name, Lille-de-Nord companies, and was located in that region of France by the same name, near Calais and the Belgian border. Many such firms were in that region. It was one of the oldest textile manufacturers in France and had always been family owned. The firm had evidently declined in value in recent years.

The president of the firm was also the head of the family, M. Alexander Bertrand. He was seventy years old and shared the management of the firm with his two sons and one son-in-law. Lavin had to be very careful

how he approached Bertrand. There must be no sugges-
tion of any suspicion of involvement in Picard's death.
He decided that the best thing to do was ask about enemies Picard might have had in pursuit of the inquiries. He called M. Bertrand, explained his intentions to
Bertrand's secretary, and was given an appointment for
the following week.

Lavin, who was a southerner, did not like northern,
industrial France. The countryside was too scarred with
factories, the cities were somewhat grimy, and he did
not care for the atmosphere of trade and business. He
had grown up in the country. The essential France was
pastoral for him. He knew that this was romantic foolishness, but he could not shake the nostalgia. By the same
token he had little patience with the Catholic France of
Charles de Gaulle who likened France in his memoir to
the "Madonna in the frescoes." Lavin had been raised
in "radical" country in small towns in which the secular
schoolmaster and the priest were antagonists. He dis-
liked and disapproved of the cluster of historical values
of royalism, religion, and authority. The family that he
was about to visit exemplified this France.

The French textile industry had become rich through
the manufacture of flax and wool. It had begun to lose
business in recent years from Asian companies and countries specializing in synthetic products that were cheaper
in the market. French manufacturers had adapted to the
competition by developing niche-oriented products like

flags, costumes, vestments, sails, awnings, ropes, medical supplies, and thermal insulation.

Lavin's homework told him that Lille-de-Nord had been slow to adapt and was suffering in the market. He wondered whether family management had perhaps been too conservative. M. Bertrand had been president for thirty years. His two sons had pushed him to modernize the plant and its equipment in the process of developing new products. The old man had resisted but had finally been persuaded to ask Picard's bank for a loan for modernization of planning and production. The shock was that the request was denied by M. Picard personally in a face-to-face meeting with M. Bertrand.

Lavin knew the story, but he decided to let Bertrand tell it himself when they met. How much would he tell, and would he leave anything out or add more? He arrived at the factory gate at ten in the morning, after taking a fast train from Paris. On the ride he saw vacant factories in the fields and could not help but lament the decline of pastoral France even though he knew that this was sentimental nostalgia. Once inside the factory he was brought into a series of offices, which began with the austere, in keeping with a factory, to a small number of reception rooms that opened upon a richly appointed executive suite in which four offices were in a circle. He was asked to wait only a few minutes until a well-groomed male secretary invited him into an inner sanctum.

M. Bertrand was standing in front of a massive desk.

He was a short muscular man, clearly in good condition for age seventy. His face was solid with eyes and a half smile that were welcoming but not exactly cordial. He invited the inspector to sit in a chair near windows overlooking the factory.

"How may I help you, Inspector?" he asked. "I know nothing about Picard's death."

"I understand this," Lavin replied. "The bank was in financial trouble, as you surely know, and I am exploring whether any of the troubles could help me find clues to his murder."

Bertrand looked at Lavin shrewdly and said nothing.

Lavin took the leap: "I understand that Picard personally denied you the loan that you requested."

He said nothing more, hoping that Bertrand would follow his lead.

Bertrand's face reddened: "That is true. It was a disgraceful thing to do after our years of association. I immediately withdrew our money from his bank and put it in a bank here in Lille."

He said this forcefully, perhaps angrily, and Lavin seized the opening to ask why Picard had rejected the request for the loan. The response was now definitely angry.

"He told me, to my face, that I had failed to keep the company up to date with the competitive market, and he doubted that we had the management and technical capacities to survive in new market conditions." He paused a moment and then added, "We are perhaps behind the times. I may have been in this seat too long and should give way to my sons. They think so. I now understand their thinking in a way that I did not a few years ago. We have lost ground, and my request to Picard was for a loan to help us gain back that ground. He should have helped us in the way that we have mutually helped each other over the years. We have always been able to get help from the bank when we needed it because he was grateful to the firm for the help that we gave him."

Bertrand stopped short, as if he had said more than he wished to say, but Lavin pressed him: "What do you mean when you say that the firm helped Picard?"

"My father helped him get started in business."

He seemed to hope to say no more, but Lavin again pressed him. "In what way?"

"My father was a friend of Picard's father and shared his political beliefs. Before the war Claude needed help getting established in business. My father helped him."

Lavin wanted to know how, and the answer cleared up a nagging puzzle.

"He gave him funds through a Swiss bank account, and Picard used that money to buy a partnership in the bank." He added, "It was not only out of friendship. He expected Claude to be good to our firm, and he was for many years, floating our bonds, lobbying the government for tariffs against foreign competition, and providing loans when we needed them.

"So, it was a great shock when he refused my request."

Bertrand relaxed, put his hands on his ample stomach, and looked at Lavin as if to say, that is all I have to tell you.

There was nothing more for Lavin to ask. The inspector could not ask anything else because there was no evidence of a crime. Picard's action seemed consistent with what Lavin understood about him. He thanked M. Bertrand and left quietly. He took a nap on the ride back to Paris.

On his return to Paris he considered the second possible case. Like the first one, it was only one story out of many possible stories that the Picards could have given him. At this time he was not thinking about the attempt on Lily's life. The two things would seem to be related, but first things first, at least for the time being. The name of the director of the Veterens de Francaise de Guerre was General Auguste Girard. He had served with distinction in the Second World War, with the Free French, in Indochina and in Algeria. He was eighty years old and might have served in World War One had he been a bit older. He was from a military family of long lineage. Lavin called Alain Picard to ask about the old man, but he did not indicate why he was interested. Alain had known Girard for many years and had been active in his pension fund.

"He is a fine old man with an impeccable military record. A good many French veterans have been neglected by successive French governments depending upon the particular politicians in power. The right has been more generous than the left, which is anti-military. Veteran benefits are expensive, and although France has a broad welfare state, their particular needs have not always been met, particularly as they have grown older. General Girard developed his organization to supplement public programs with private sources of financial help to pensioners."

Alain could not imagine that his younger brother would refuse to help such a worthy cause, but he warned Lavin to be careful not to even suggest any connection between Girard's organization and his brother's murder. He added,

"Girard is very hot-tempered. He was never that way in the Army because he directed his temper at the enemy and politicians, whom he despised. He is extraordinarily loyal to his veterans, as if they had all served under him, just as he was to those he actually led. So, be careful not to rouse his temper."

Lavin listened carefully, as he always did, and developed his strategy accordingly. Girard's organization was in the Paris telephone book, and he called and asked to speak with the general. Lavin identified himself and explained that he was pursuing an investigation. The assistant who responded said that the general was away and that she would call back after she talked with him. She called back a few days later to say that the general was at his country home in Brittany and did not wish to talk with the inspector until he returned to Paris after Christmas. Lavin was not in the least bit satisfied with the answer and asked her to tell the general that he was investigating the murder of Claude Picard and wanted to talk with him as soon as possible. After another interval of several days, word came back that General Girard would see Lavin at his home in Brittany at the inspector's convenience. A date was eventually set, and Lavin got ready for the meeting.

The train ride to Brittany was through beautiful, green rolling country, and the ride gave Lavin time to think about the interview. He was looking for a suspect on the basis of what de Frontenac had told him, but this case might turn out like the last, a grievance without any trace of a crime. He thought that he might try to provoke the general into a temper to see if that produced anything, but he would be diplomatic and careful at first.

The general's home was a handsome stone house set on the side of a hill overlooking a deep valley. It was not far from the ocean, and fog enveloped the house as he approached it. It was an area of comfortable country homes; some were retirees, and others were prosperous farmers. The taxi took him up a gravel drive to the front portico of stone pillars. A man dressed in military uniform greeted him at the door and invited him into a corridor leading into a sitting room with a large open fireplace, leather chairs, and a number of paintings and photographs of military encampments and officers from long past. Windows looked out on the valley. The general was standing in front of the windows.

He walked forward and extended his hand, introducing himself as General Auguste Girard, and invited Lavin to a chair in front of the fireplace. It was cold, and a small fire was burning. He was tall, easily six feet or more, with excellent posture. His chest was in front of his shoulders in a way that would enhance the display of military medals. He was dressed in a tweed suit.

"I cannot think why you would wish to see me, M. Lavin, but I am at your service."

Lavin thanked the general for his willingness to meet and added, "I know that you and Claude Picard had a disagreement that I would like to explore with you."

The provocation brought color to Girard's face. "Surely you do not suspect me of murder?"

"I have no reason to do so," replied the inspector, "but someone may have been angered by M. Picard's refusal to give to your fund. I thought perhaps that you could help me in that regard."

Girard did not relax. If anything, he stiffened in composure.

"I represent honorable men who served their country, often under difficult conditions, and much of the time, without the political or public support that their missions demanded. I will not let you impugn my cause or those who serve it."

Lavin knew the answer coming but then asked,

"Did you talk with Claude Picard about your request for a gift for your foundation?"

The general did not answer at first.

"I wrote him a letter in which I set out the terms of a gift and its purposes. After too long a time I received a routine answer from a bank official that my request was under consideration. After some weeks I heard nothing. I called de Frontenac, and he could tell me nothing but promised to find out and call me back. This did not happen. I waited two more weeks and then called for an appointment with Picard. After all, I had known him for years, never well, but socially. The bank had contributed to our fund in the past, and I could not understand the delay or imagine a refusal to help. The secretary called and told me that he could not see me for at least two weeks.

"I decided that I would go see him at home. I did not wish to force myself into his office at the bank. I went in the evening, about six at dusk. There were few lights on in the house when I rang the bell, but he answered the door and invited me in. He led the way to his study on the side of the house, telling me that it was the butler's night off and that the cook had gone home. He invited me to a chair in front of his desk, and he sat behind the desk. Of course, he knew what I wanted, but he let me pose my request again. When I had done so, he said, without pausing or reflecting, that he would have done so ordinarily but that he had held up all charitable donations for a time because both he and the bank were in financial trouble. He did not provide any details.

"I was not prepared to accept this. I knew that he had made a donation to the Paris Opera, of which he was a long-standing patron. 'Surely,' I said, 'your past political associations,' by which I meant his support for French interests in Indochina and Algeria, 'should require you to be generous to the soldiers who had fought fruitlessly in these wars.'

"He did not like this at all. He rose up from his desk, came around, and stood in front of me as if to intimidate me. This was his style; he was a bully. I stood up and put my face in his and told him that he was not a patriot, and I said 'patriot' in a raised voice. He told me to back off, but I did not. He then pushed me hard in the chest. My feet were firm, and I pushed him back. He fell and hit his head on one of the heavy bookends on his desk. His body slumped to the floor. It all happened too fast. I had no intention of hurting him. He was alive after he fell because I took his pulse. I then called the police and gave the address and asked for the ambulance. I left the house quickly, leaving the front door unlocked.

"I am telling you this because I have been in agony over my actions. I suppose that I would have come to the police to confess sooner or later because the guilt is too great. My push was not intended to hurt him, but it did kill him. I should have stayed for the police and told them the story. I am even more culpable now because I ran away."

He walked across the room and sat down in what seemed be a favorite chair and looked at Lavin. The inspector went over and sat next to him. He had not expected anything so dramatic. And yet, the facts hung together in a clear, simple way. He had solved the crime, if it was a crime, by indirection. Lavin looked thoughtfully and even sympathetically at Girard and said,

"You could be charged with manslaughter perhaps, certainly not with murder. The killing could be portrayed by a lawyer as accidental. In that case, your only offense would be leaving the scene of a crime, if it was a crime. In any event, your reputation as a man of honor would be damaged, probably permanently. You would have to give up your public work on behalf of veterans, although you could continue to work privately."

The general replied, "I am relieved in my conscience. I have no family left, and so my loss of honor will die with me. What do you suggest I do now?"

Lavin thought a moment and then said words that he had not anticipated and could hardly believe himself saying,

"I will return to Paris today. I expect to see you at the Sûreté at eleven in the morning on Monday. You will make your statement, as you have to me, before the prosecutor to whom I report, and he will make a decision about what to do. I think that he will release you on bond and assign a trial date. The press need not know about the matter until it comes to trial."

The general seemingly accepted all that Lavin had said, but he had simply nodded his head in agreement and then closed his eyes as the inspector left the room. Lavin felt that he had done the right thing in not arresting Girard and taking him to jail in handcuffs. He had solved the crime but could not rest easy because of one question: Who had tried to kill Lily and why?

On Sunday morning he read this headline in his paper:

"Distinguished general shot himself last night."

It made sense to him, although he regretted it.

Chapter 10

Who would want to kill Lily de Frontenac and why? The answer would seem to be related to her new position as bank president. But Girard could not have been involved. That was not the nature of his crime. Where was Lavin to look now? He made an appointment to see Lily and Paul at their home in order to talk informally. They lived in a spacious house not far from where her father had lived. They were both intellectuals of a mandarin kind, that is, very well-educated people who moved in elite circles. In their case the circles were respectable conservative literary groups closely tied to government and politics. They associated freely with high officials and advisors no matter who was president of France. These people were not like American conservatives. They were well connected to finance and industry that also believed in a strong national government. This was a French tradition

of long-standing not usually found in the United States or
even Britain. They had become friends of John and Julie
Page on the basis of past associations. The two Americans
understood the French couple better than Lily and Paul
understood them for neither of them had any experience
of American life and had never been to the United States.
On more than one occasion John, who had kept in touch
with Lavin, had assured him of the honesty and reliability
of the French couple.

The de Frontenac's home was large with rooms for
three children, servants, and an office for each parent.
They often worked at home with easy access to each
other, even though their offices in the bank were next
door. Lavin wondered how much actual authority the
two vice presidents of the bank had. He asked about
Jean Lucet, and they told him that Lucet had been made
vice president in charge of foreign investment, fitting his
background.

He asked them for their ideas about who might want
to kill Lily or remove her from the bank, as if these questions could have different answers. Neither one could
think of any enemies, personal or political. She had been
a well-regarded journalist. Her political and economic
ideas were right of center but moderate. She had always
had many friends and could not think of any personal
enemies.

Lavin then asked about decisions that she, as president of the bank, might have made that would cause

anger against her. Again, she could think of nothing. Questions about the Spanish and Moroccan banks had been resolved. Lavin asked if the investments of their bank overseas could have raised any problems. This did bring a matter to mind. Lily told him that the bank had recently helped the national government of Algeria release its own bonds onto financial markets. The fees were good. Jean Lucet was now in charge of such investments, and he might know something about the Algerian matter. It would be good to talk with him about his work in general because he had learned the North African terrain quite well.

Lucet was happy to be at work in the family institution. His office was filled with paper and the air of activity. Secretaries kept rushing in and out with papers for him to sign. At last he settled back during a lull and responded to Lavin's question.

"We have not had any negative reactions to our investments. But you know there are political movements critical of governmental and business authorities in North Africa. The Salifist and Muslim Brotherhood movements in Egypt are the strongest such forces, but they are underground. We have recently assisted the government of Algeria in marketing bonds, and there are strong Islamist groups hostile to that government, particularly the Salvation Front. I suppose that you might make further inquiries in that direction. I would be glad to help with names and information if you wish."

Lavin thanked him and decided to take a new tack. He called Inspector François Benoît of the Marseille police and asked him if he had discovered anything about the Corsican investment that the Ramirez brothers had been concerned about. The answer was that nothing was known because nothing had been done. It was not a priority for the Marseille police. Lavin went out on a limb and suggested that there might be a connection with a murder in Paris, and this got Benoît's attention.

He then called John Page to ask him if they could talk about Islamist terrorism in North Africa. He was not sufficiently specific so Page asked him to narrow the topic a bit. Lavin explained a possible Corsican connection with Algerian terrorists, and Page said that he would be happy to look into things. He also reminded Lavin about the threat that he had received from the letters he had initially written to people in Paris. Nothing learned so far had answered that question. Could Picard himself have sent it, as well as his cordial reply? But, if so, why? The answer might help Lavin in some way.

Time passed. Lavin eventually heard from François Benoît that the police in Marseille suspected the people in Corsica to be a money laundering operation. They had no business of their own except money exchange. Large amounts of cash moved in and out of their office every day. Such flows of money were difficult to track, and it would take time to do so. They would keep Lavin informed and asked him to wait until they knew more. He was stymied again.

Then lightning struck. An attempt was made on the life of a second bank president in Paris, and a day or two later, a key official in the Ministry of Finance was shot dead in the back patio of his home. It did not take Lavin long to make the necessary connection. The second bank had also assisted the government of Algeria send bonds to the market, and the official in the Ministry of Finance had helped pave the way for both bank actions with the government of Algeria. He got on the telephone and asked John Page to help him. Whoever these people were, they were still active. Lily had not been a 'one off.' The Corsican affair might or might not be important, and he set it aside for the moment to ask about Algeria directly.

Page and Lavin settled down for a weekend of education and discussion about Algeria. Lavin was deliberately apolitical as a matter of policy, not wishing to be caught up in French politics in his work in any way. He had never voted, for example. So it was no surprise that he required education in North African politics. They settled down on a rainy Saturday afternoon in Lavin's apartment for a broad sweep of Algerian history. Page had written a short book about De Gaulle's actions in nineteen fifty nine to separate France from its Algerian colony.

"De Gaulle came power after a long absence from French politics and became the president of the new Fifth Republic. He seemed to be the only answer to the turmoil and virtual civil war in the French colony of Algeria. He confronted a revolt of French generals and the threat of an invasion of France from Algeria and once they were overcome Algeria was given its independence.

"The new government of Algeria consisted of the elite from the party of independence that had defeated the French, the FLN (Front de Liberation Nationale).

"I did research there in the nineteen sixties. The government was not democratic in any procedural sense. Elections were plebiscites in which it was returned to office regularly. It was a popular dictatorship. Over the course of time the government's 'revolutionary' fervor had cooled, and it had developed political arteriosclerosis. Popular resentments and antagonisms had developed, and then, along with other currents in the Moslem world, a politics of Islamic extremism developed. This was in response to the corrupt, unresponsive governing one-party state. But there was something more, which was a politics of Islamic identity. Algerian nationalism at independence was inspired by Western political ideology, especially Marxist ideas, which were turned against Western imperialism and capitalism. Such protests helped prepare the way for a total rejection of Western society according to Islamic principles.

"The difficulty was that the old revolutionaries, once in power, were at odds with the new revolutionaries who wished to reject their 'Western' ideologies and overthrow them in a total rejection of Western beliefs and values.

The Salvation Front was the political movement that represented the new politics of protest. It operated in the
open in the 1970s and 1980s, becoming active in left-
wing student politics in universities, among conservative
women who began to wear the veil, and in the oratory
of strident mullahs. The government made a mistake,
in terms of its own interests, in the mid-1980s by permit-
ting the Front to contest in the general election to the
national legislative assembly. Much to official surprise,
the Islamists won a majority of seats in a protest vote.
The old revolutionaries were not going to permit the
new revolution to threaten everything they had fought
so many years for, and the government canceled the verdict and declared martial law. Order was created at the
price of disorder in disruption and violence, followed by
repression.

"I was able to interview many Islamist leaders and have
some contacts there should you want to explore these
questions."

This history gave Lavin the context he needed in
which to work. Both he and John assumed that the attacks in France might have been intended as reprisals for
financial aid to the government of Algeria. It made sense
to look at the Salvation Front, but they would need help.
Lavin wanted to pursue a possible Corsican connection
with Algeria and he called François Benoît in Marseille
again, urging action. Benoît offered to help, and so Lavin
and John went to Marseille immediately and sat down

with Benoît. If people in Corsica were laundering money from the Salvation Front, this would tell them a great deal about what to do next. Lavin was following hunches, as he had been doing right along only to uncover false leads, and this could be another one, but he had to try.

Benoît suggested that they pursue an Algerian end as well. Would the Algerian police know about how the Salvation Front might be able to send its money abroad for profit? He knew the Prefect of Police in Algiers, Major Walid Kamel, and called him as they were sitting there. He put on the speaker phone, and the four men talked in French.

"We have put the more vocal and volatile leaders of the Salvation Front in jail for a time, but they will be released eventually. Their activities will be banned for the future. The government cannot just stamp them out because they speak for a good many Algerians. This is an issue for the government. I only do my duty as a policeman. You are looking for an assassin, but that could be anyone the Front selected from among many possible killers. I don't see how I can help you."

John Page spoke,

"I know a member of the Front who is politically radical but does not believe in violence. His name is Rayan Anis. Do you know him?"

"Yes, we do know him. He was not arrested but is confined at home for the duration of the crisis. Do you want to talk with him? This may be difficult because he is not permitted to use the telephone or communicate with anyone other than his immediate family. That rule applies to all Front members who are not in jail. I cannot make exceptions."

Kamel's stubbornness was getting on Lavin's nerves. He blustered out,

"See here, Major. We are investigating an important crime against the government of France. An important official has been killed by an assassin, and two private citizens have been nearly killed. We cannot permit this to continue. We cannot wait for your crisis to be resolved. I want permission to talk with this man, Anis, right now. If you do not give it immediately, I will have no choice but to speak with the French Foreign Office."

After a silence, the major replied, "All right, but you will have to come here to talk with him, and only one of you. We do not want the Front to know any of our investigations. Who will you send, and when?"

Lavin and John looked at each other. One was a policeman experienced in interviewing all sorts of people. The other was a professor with limited experience, but John was fluent in Arabic, understood Arab politics, and had talked often with Arabs from all walks of life. He had not known many members of the Salvation Front, but he knew Rayan Anis from his past field research on Islamist movements in North Africa. Anis had the reputation as one who believed in constitutional democracy. But for that reason he was not a member of the inner core of leadership of the Salvation Front. He was, however, used by Front leaders when they wished to communicate with the government of Algeria. John spoke first,

"I will go to Algiers. But let's not tell my wife."

Lavin was very reluctant to let him go without a bodyguard and insisted to Kamel that John must be well protected in Algiers. Assurances were given, a date was set, and travel plans would be forwarded. This plan was contingent on Anis's willingness to talk with John. They asked him to make the appeal that they were seeking to curb possible violence by the Salvation Front.

Back at their hotel John thought better of his rashness and called Julie to tell her of his plan. He would be in Algiers for one day and return the next morning, and he would be protected by the police every minute, even in his hotel room.

She was most strongly opposed,

"Look here, John Franklin Page. Think of your children and grandchildren whom you have not even seen because they have not yet been born. You owe me and your children the obligation to stay alive because we love you. Throw all that stuff out the window, and come home now."

Lavin could hear Julie's voice. He threw up his arms in a shrug and put his thumbs down. "It is She Who Must be Obeyed," he said with a smile.

John agreed. But what were they to do now? They did not have to wait long for an answer. The Foreign Ministry of France decided that a delegation would visit Algiers to investigate the murder of a high-ranking French official and attempts on the lives of two French citizens. It was assumed in the ministry that the financial help to the Algerian government was involved. This was not publicly announced, but there was to be a simultaneous French police investigation in concert with the official delegation.

Lavin was notified because of his current inquiry about Algeria.

He knew that he had to get John Page as part of the official delegation as an expert on political Islam. This would not be easy because France had its own experts. Why push in an Anglo-Saxon? John's acquaintance with Rayan Anis was a good excuse but the ministry had to be persuaded, and it would help if a French colleague of John's might join him in the effort. John could think of two or three scholars as possibilities. They were all on the faculty of the Sorbonne. But only one, in his judgment, was suited for a clandestine mission. He was Jacques Voegeli, an expert on terrorism, whom John knew only slightly and largely by reputation.

When they returned to Paris, he called Voegeli, told him that he was also at the Sorbonne and wondered if they might get together. He said that it was a professional visit to talk shop. Voegeli had an office near the Sorbonne on a side street. It was large with big windows and room for several tables covered with Arab newspapers and magazines. A number of file cabinets were crammed with folios. Voegeli had left one open and taken out a file on John's publications. He was a small birdlike man with a sharp Gallic nose and most acute eyes. He welcomed John as a colleague whose work he respected. They were part of a small fraternity of scholars on North Africa. After some small talk about John's life, current project and Voegeli's research, there was a pause, and John decided to plunge into his topic.

"I am delighted to get acquainted, but I must be honest. I come with an ulterior motive."

He told the Frenchman how he had come to be involved with Lavin and the sequence of events that had led to his present visit.

"They want me to go to Algiers as an adjunct to the official delegation but thought it best that a French expert be enlisted as well. Why use me and not a Frenchman, particularly if publicity follows our adventure?"

Voegeli smiled and asked him to go on.

"We do not know if the Salvation Front is responsible for these attacks, but it is more than plausible to assume so. The thought is that I might be able to find out something from Rayan Anis about them. I know Anis but not well. He is opposed to violence in politics and might be willing to help us. We do not know how he feels about the current political situation in Algeria. He must be hostile to the current martial law and the suppression of his own party. However, he might also favor new kinds of political reform above ground."

Voegeli said that this was a realistic estimate worth exploring, adding,

"The Front appears to have split between those who have responded to the government's actions with a renewed commitment to violence and those, perhaps like Anis, who wish to practice democratic politics. The difficulty is that the government of Algeria enjoys a monopoly of power and does not want to share it with any Islamist party, no matter how democratic.

"Do you want me to go with you to talk with Anis?"

John thought that this was a great idea and they talked for the rest of the morning about Algerian politics and had lunch at the Great Mosque, which was nearby.

Chapter 11

The relevant officials in the Ministry of Foreign Affairs had their eyes on future talks with Algerian officials. They gave approval for the Page and Voegeli roles as advisors and did not consider that either man would play an independent role. Indeed, it was not suggested by the police officials who won the ministry's approval for them as advisors to official negotiators. For this reason approaches to Anis had to be informal and carried out at lower levels. Police officials in Algiers had to cooperate because they were to protect the two professors.

John had fired rifles in the army but never at anyone. Lavin took him to a police rifle range for instruction in the use of a pistol. He was to take one with him, even though he would surely be checked by Anis's people before any interview. Lavin wanted him to have it during the remainder of his time in Algiers. He was shown how to use the gun at close range, twenty paces or less, in case he was accosted by surprise. He shot the weapon pretty well. The hardest thing was to get it out of the shoulder holster under his coat. He kept thinking of all the detective movies he had seen as a boy. Cowboys reached down and drew. It was harder for a plainclothes policeman, which he suddenly had become. Voegeli needed no training since he had been in the French infantry during the war in Algeria. The experience had stimulated his academic interest in terrorism.

Inspector Walid Kamel was responsible for contacting Anis about a visit from the two scholars. He was told that they were assisting in the investigation of the Paris attacks. They had decided that it was best to explain their purpose from the outset. They also asked if Voegeli might come as well. Telling Anis their purpose was a gamble that could have failed, but Rayan Anis sent back a message that he would talk with Page and Voegeli secretly in a location other than his home. He would contact them.

They went to Algiers along with the official French delegation and waited. They had briefed the official delegation at length about the Salvation Front, and there was nothing for John and Jacques to do except wait in their hotel for a word from Anis. They dared not go out in the city for fear of being seen by Salvation Front informants. This might have scared Anis off for fear of action against him by others in the movement.

A call came from Walid Kamel that they were to be

in John Page's hotel room at 11:00 p.m. on Saturday. The police would take them to Anis. There was a knock on the door at that time, and two men searched them for weapons and took them down a freight elevator and through a back door into an alley and a police car. They drove for some time, and Voegeli, who knew Algiers better than John, recognized nothing. After about half an hour the car entered a garage, and the door was closed behind it. They wondered if they were in a trap. Neither of their minders said a word.

They climbed a staircase in the garage that led to a steel door. One of the men knocked on the interior wooden door. There was no audible reply, but the door opened to a dark corridor, which they entered. This gave way to another door, which also required unlocking from within, to a room of sofas and chairs. Three men were in the room. John recognized Anis and acknowledged him with a nod but said nothing. Even sitting down, he was a tall man with a muscular build and what one would call a strong face, with large jaws, high cheekbones, and an expressive mouth. He wore a loose-fitting robe, but without a head-scarf, which was unusual. His hair was black.

John had met him about ten years before, and he had not changed in appearance. He judged that Anis was about fifty. The two police escorts withdrew to the side of the room, leaving John and Voegeli standing in front of the three men. The other two men did not move but stared at them so closely that John decided they were bodyguards.

Anis finally spoke, in very good French: "I remember you, Professor Page, when you were here a few years ago. We met in an interview about the Salvation Front. You seemed to understand the politics of Algeria quite well. You were not a naïve social scientist exploring a subject from ignorance."

John answered, "Thank you for the compliment. I am a poke and soak researcher who tries to understand reality from the ground up."

Anis then spoke to Voegeli, "You look at the dark side of our movement. This is a side that I reject. It has been toughened by the government as it has outlawed the party. I believe that the government should have permitted us to govern. We are now at an impasse between extremes."

He had not invited them to sit down but then motioned to John that they were to sit, asking, "Your request of me is most unusual. You want me to lead you to assassins. Why should I do this?"

John answered, "We thought that you might cooperate in curbing an outbreak of violence in this conflict. If assassins can be caught and punished, it might cause less killing. The resolution of the current political crisis is beyond our competence. We seek only this one goal."

Anis looked at the two men thoughtfully. "What makes you think that I would know about these things? My responsibilities in the Front are strictly political. I am not likely to know anything about killing anyone. Such matters are handled very secretively."

"We understand," said Voegeli, "but we hoped that you might lead us to someone who could give us information."

Anis said nothing for some time and continued to appraise them.

"You would not be able to find out what you want to know from police informants. I do not know of any assassins, but I can tell you of an organization that puts them up for hire. The Front is not willing to turn any of its operatives into professional killers. If they need such a person, they might approach these people. I doubt if the police here know of this organization. Its headquarters are in Corsica, which, as you know, is a nest of international intrigue. I will give you the name of an informant in Algiers. This may or may not help you. He knows about the group that some of the more ruthless men in the Front have favored from time to time, although it has been some years because we have been trying to attain political legitimacy in Algeria. The assassinations in Paris seem like senseless revenge to me, but they are strikes against the government here in the eyes of those who ask for them."

He then stared at the men with a hard, penetrating look.

"I am taking a personal risk to help you. If this conversation is discovered by the wrong people my life will be at risk because they will not hesitate to kill me. Your own lives would also be in danger, no matter where you live. I assume that this meeting is secret."

They assured him that was the case, and he rose and promptly left the room. They were eventually led out the way they entered. Anis had handed John Page the address on a piece of paper written in English. The policemen in the room were not to see it. Once back at their hotel John and Voegeli began to discuss what to do.

They decided that they would share the information only with Lavin for the time being. The delegation of the French ministry was in discussion with the Algerian government about how to ameliorate the conflicts with the Salvation Front. The Algerian police did want information about assassins, and they raised the question of how to help them when they talked with Lavin the next day.

"This is a French matter," said Lavin the next morning, "but we must work with the police here in Algiers since the source may be here. I will talk with the Prefect of Police today and see what he thinks. We will need specialized help from Paris. The best thing for the two of you is to go back home and await word from me."

There was really nothing more for John and Voegeli to do, so they flew back to Paris but both were disappointed to be dismissed from an intriguing story. They had gotten a taste of intrigue. It was some time before John heard from Lavin, and the message was more courtesy than information. Lavin said, "We are working with the police in Corsica and making slow progress, but this will take

time. Be close at hand, for we may need you again in case
something develops again in North Africa."

These cryptic words were puzzling and tantalizing.
John could not believe the twists and turns the story
had taken from the visit that he and Julie had made to
Provence in the early fall. It was now December with cold,
foggy, and rainy days. They would go home at the latest in
August, and it would be nice if the story would end before
that time. He did not expect to play a personal role again,
but it had been exciting and he wanted to stay close to
events if they unfolded to a conclusion. Walid Kamel,
Lavin, and Benoît had contacted the informant whose
name Anis provided. He was not a police informant at all,
but a man who followed underground news about politics
and used it to his own advantage. The government had
been his primary client. He was not with the Salvation
Front, but he knew many people connected with the activities of the Front. They told him that they were policemen and threatened to put him out of business unless
he helped them. That would have meant cutting off his
clients. They could not be sure that he would know what
they wanted to know or that he would not mislead them,
but deliberate deception would also be punished.

He gave them a name in Corsica of someone who had
been used by the organization identified by Anis, but
would say no more. François Benoît knew colleagues in
Corsica, so they went there and gave the name to a police official. He stared at them and asked how on earth

they came up with the name. After they explained the full story to him, he was still amazed. He asked for a few days to explore the man's record and then met with them again.

"We have been watching this man for some time. He is a very unusual criminal. We have been looking at him on a possible charge of smuggling drugs into France. He plays the oboe in the Corsican symphony orchestra. He was also in the French army in Algeria. He goes to North Africa often and knows many people there. There have been a number of reports about him from police informants but nothing definite. But we can connect him with two of the attacks in Paris that concern you. He was in Paris on both occasions, and in both cases he used false passports. We did not link him with those attacks until just now, after we have heard from you. His orchestra was not performing, and he had time to himself. We have investigated his smuggling connections but are not ready to act on that now."

A fallow period followed in which the police watched the man carefully, wiretapped his telephone, and read his mail. Then he made plans to fly to Cairo, using a false name. He went to the airport with that passport, and they arrested him before he could board the plane. He was taken to the police station and grilled. He would admit nothing, but a search of his apartment found several powerful rifles. They also found an address book with home addresses of the two men who were shot in Paris. This evidence was very incriminating, but he asked for a lawyer and would say nothing. There was no evidence linking him to Lily de Frontenac. He could not be charged with the attempt to kill her. There was one address in Tangier with nothing attached to it, not even a telephone number.

Lavin decided that something had to be done about it so he called Inspector Ahmed Mourad of the Tangier police and asked if they could come there to inquire. Mourad agreed. The address was of a large apartment house in a middle-class section of the city. He would do nothing until they arrived. Both Benoît and Lavin went to see Mourad. He was an experienced policeman, and they settled down to talk. His people had been watching the apartment house, but many people came in and out every day, and they did not have an apartment number. They had obtained a list of all owners of apartments, but this could tell them nothing by itself. A slow process of working down the list of two hundred names eliminated a good many people, by age and occupation. It was not likely that a bank manager with four children would be a criminal. There were thirty single people.

The winnowing began again. The names were Moroccan, French, and Spanish. They decided to check the ten Moroccan names first. None had criminal records. They were all employed. There was one musician, and that caught their attention because of their Corsican musician, named Karim Ali. Of course they could be friends. This man had played in a French symphony orchestra in Bordeaux for some years but had left and was giving private cello lessons. He had made trips to Paris in recent months, including the day when the attempt was made on Lily's life. But this could tell them nothing by itself. However, he went other places as well. He had been in Cairo, Nairobi, Baghdad, and London within the last five years.

Lavin called Scotland Yard to see if they knew anything about him. He learned that the suspect was a strong, vocal supporter of a Moroccan mullah in London, Omar Khaled, who was the usual inflammatory preacher with a largely immigrant following, but no violence was linked to his name or his mosque. Ali had supported the mosque financially and was thought to be a personal friend of Khaled. This was not very good evidence of any wrongdoing. They eventually found that Ali's mother was Algerian. This could tell nothing by itself.

The search for other possible suspects seemed to go nowhere. Then they had a break. The Corsican assassin confessed to the two killings and implicated Ali as another professional assassin. They were friends and the Moroccan address in his book had meant nothing by itself, but the confession did. Ali had traveled to Paris a few days before the attempt to kill Lily and had left the next morning. He traveled without weapons, suggesting the existence of accomplices in Paris.

The Tangier police agreed to detain Ali for questioning,

and they were able to talk with him. He was like a rock. He denied everything and would not talk. He had come to Paris to attend a concert, and he showed them ticket stubs. Only a man covering his tracks would have done this. A careful review of his travel schedule confirmed killings in those cities and countries during each of his trips. The victims were either politicians or businessmen.

They withdrew while the local police worked on him in ways that they wished not to know about. A call then came that he had confessed. He had been hired and paid to go to Paris to kill Lily. He had surveyed her neighborhood, seen that two households were seemingly away, and picked a spot from which to fire into her back patio. Paris accomplices had supplied the rifle and an automobile ride to and from the house. He fired only one shot and left when she disappeared from sight. He took the plane back to Tangier the next morning.

The confession was incomplete without the story of who hired him. He insisted that he knew only the man's name, no details about him. The name of the intermediary was not anyone the police were familiar with in their underworld, and they were baffled. The assassin had been paid cash in a café near the bank in which Jean Lucet had worked.

Lavin was sceptical that the attack on Lily was motivated by the same attacks on the Ministry of Finance official and the other bank president, because it had taken place before Lily's bank had assisted the Algerian government with the issue of bonds. He had a tangible lead for once and called Edouard Lesage, the president of the bank in Tangier, and asked him if there was any record of a withdrawal from his bank for the amount paid to the assssin at the time in question. Lesage inquired of the bookkeepers and told Lavin that there was a roughly similar amount of withdrawal a few weeks before the attempt on Lily's life. The money had been drawn from Jean Lucet's account.

Lavin could not believe that Lucet was guilty. It contradicted his assessment of the man. Still, he had to face the situation. He called Lucet for an appointment, and once in the banker's office he confronted him with his story and the evidence.

Lucet looked at Lavin in horror. "Inspector, this is a nightmare. I never withdrew such a sum from my bank account, and I never wanted to or tried to kill Lily. This is a terrible mistake of some kind."

"But how do you explain the withdrawal of the money from your bank account?" asked Lavin.

"My bank book shows no such withdrawal," protested Lucet. He produced his bank records from a file in his office, and there was no such sum for the period in question.

Lavin had to consider that Lucet's bank book could have been altered to conceal a withdrawal. He had to decide what to do on the spot.

"All right, we will leave the question open for now, but you must not leave Paris and must call me every Monday and Friday to tell me where you are and what you are doing."

Lucet was visibly worried, almost panicked. Lavin wondered, Is this because he is guilty or because he is innocent ? Lavin made judgments quickly, as he had done with General Girard. He told Lucet,

"I will do nothing for the present. Think about what you might do to clear your name. Who might want to divert blame from themselves to you?"

With this he left a frightened man and went home to his wife. Perhaps she could help clarify his confusion. She cooked him a good meal, and he enjoyed two glasses of red wine before they settled down to talk. She had always been his best adviser.

"Everything that you know about Jean Lucet tells you that he is not a murderer. Why would he want to kill his sister? Her murder would not get him into the bank. In fact, it would probably cast suspicion on him. Why don't you ask yourself: Who would have a motive to cast doubt on Jean and away from themselves?"

She persisted, "You need better evidence about Jean's bank account in Tangier. You only have the word of the bank, and someone there may have tried to mislead you."

Sylvine knew that her husband had surely thought of these things, but she had discovered that she could reinforce his own good, half-articulated thoughts and pick out the best possibilities. She had learned to be a good detective by living with him for so many years.

He had the report from Lesage but could not challenge the bank president directly. He needed evidence from the bank records themselves, but how to do it? He called Ahmed Mourad, the police inspector in Tangier, and asked for assistance. It was a ticklish point because private bank accounts may not be examined by the police except with a warrant and the suspicion of a crime. Lavin wished to avoid such rash action because it might warn anyone who had deliberately altered Lucet's account. He was asking Mourad to break the law in the interest of the law. But policemen may at times proceed by indirection without flouting the law. They only bend it a little. Mourad had an informant in the bank who could see without suspicion. He told Lavin that it would take a few days.

In due course he called back, "There is no record of a payment of that sum from Lucet's account during the time that he worked for the bank. He spent money on his apartment and simple maintenance of his other needs, and little else. There was no attempt to alter the bank's record about Lucet. The report that came to you was evidently false."

Now what was Lavin to do? Lesage may have received a false report from an unknown conspirator, or was the offense from Lesage himself? And, if so, why? The detective decided that he needed to know about Edouard Lesage's history, and he set to work. It was not difficult to develop the story. Lesage had a modest bourgeois family background. His university education had been interrupted by the war and he never returned, but went to work for Picard's bank as a junior cashier. He left to join a Paris accounting firm. He had gradually worked his way up to a position of responsibility in the firm, one of whose principal clients was Claude Picard's bank. It was not known whether he had ever met Picard. He moved to an export-import company in the 1960s and began extensive work in North Africa. This led to the offer of the presidency of the bank in Tangier in 1970. He had initiated the offer to invest in Picard's bank before Picard was killed, and negotiations were continuing. He had hired Lucet without any idea that Lucet was part of Picard's family but had been cooperative in Lucet's disclosure of his identity and membership in the Paris bank.

Why would he blame the attempt to kill Lily on Lucet? Lavin reasoned that if he wanted to remove Lily and Lucet from the scene, he would have an opportunity to take over the bank. De Frontenac might not be much of an obstacle. Still it all seemed far-fetched to Lavin. Was an investment or even the control of a bank worth two lives?

Lavin also discovered that Lesage was sympathetic with nationalist causes in North Africa. He had been a fierce supporter of Algerian and Moroccan independence and was known as a critic of the authoritarian governments that had resulted. This conviction could cause him to oppose companies and banks in France that supported those governments. Lavin wondered if there could be a connection between such politics and the attack on Lily.

He flew to Tangier and made an appointment to see Lesage. After he walked into the president's office, he blurted out,

"The report that you gave me about Lucet's payment to a person unknown is false. Could it have come to you in that way?"

"I do not know, but I can find out and let you know," Lesage replied.

"I think that you concocted it for reasons of you own," replied Lavin, going out on a limb.

Lesage's face became fiery red, and he replied in anger,

"How could you make such a claim?"

"Because I know for a fact that the information that came to you reported no such expenditure. You must have made it up and lied to me. Furthermore, I did not tell you the amount of the payment to the assassin, but you used that figure, which you did not know, as the sum for Lucet's withdrawal."

Lesage was quiet and stared at Lavin.

"If you want to talk to me any more, you will have to talk to my lawyer."

"Fine, but we can do it in the police station. We are going to go downstairs, get into a cab, and go there. If you agree to go quietly, I will cooperate with an arrest there. Otherwise, I will arrest you now, and you can go downstairs in handcuffs."

Lesage went quietly. The Moroccan police were

cooperative. Lavin had discussed the possibility before he went to see Lesage. After Lesage spent a few days in jail, his lawyer asked for bail, but the Tangier judge would not give it. He was sent to France to be arraigned and wait for trial. Under the pressure of imprisonment he weakened and confessed to hiring the assassin to attack Lily. He claimed that his intention was to frighten her so that she would be more inclined to leave her leadership of the bank of the bank. He wanted to take control of the bank in which he had once worked as a young man by buying a substantial share.

Lavin called Lucet immediately and relieved the young man's mind.

He then moved to other assignments, and Lesage was eventually sentenced to ten years for his crime. Lavin thought it was too soft a sentence, but his job was to catch criminals, not to judge them.

It had all begun with John Page's simple questions about his mother and uncle. The story unfolded in unforeseen and unpredictable ways. Lavin had seen it happen again and again. He went to court to hear the verdict and then went home to his wife for a good meal and two glasses of red wine.

There was one unresolved question, however. Who had warned John Page not to pursue friends of his mother and uncle in Paris in the 1920s? There was no answer. Lavin decided that he would let the mystery continue.